D1561685

UNSUNG
HEROES

Chloe!
Hope you enjoy!
Besides acting like I am 11 years
old I do teach, do pull ups, + write
books! I promise I'll always be
a child the couple times I see
you a year! Love
Kyle G

Kyle Gurkovich

ISBN: 1517000777
ISBN 13: 9781517000776
Library of Congress Control Number: 2015915821
CreateSpace Independent Publishing Platform
North Charleston, South Carolina

To my family and friends –
Thanks for always supporting me with my crazy
endeavors!

TABLE OF CONTENTS

CHAPTER ONE

Chicago, USA—May 23, 1924

Cathal crouched behind a 1922 Lincoln Sedan, peering around the side to check on his targets. He saw two men conversing together in pinstripe black suits, armed with machine guns. He knew he was at the right place; he could just feel it.

It was about two in the morning—a normal time for the Conti mob family to be going over their usual shipments of alcohol, which usually went unnoticed by the everyday people of the great city of Chicago. Cathal remembered reading that this branch of the mob most often did this type of business at this time of night. This was because Prohibition was in effect.

From his position, he could see the entrance where they were unloading the wooden crates into the warehouse, right along the back of the dock. The brick warehouse had seen better days. The outside looked very worn and unkempt. At one time, the company that ran the building took great pride in its appearance in the neighborhood and kept the outside in perfect condition. Since then, it had been bought out and now was used strictly for moving illegal material in and out. The appearance was of no concern to whoever now owned the building. Cathal peered back around the back end of the car to see if he could listen for the object he was seeking—a crate carrying an object that would lead him one step closer to saving the world he so loved.

"Make sure you place the marked crate in the don's office. He specifically requested it to be there when he arrives," one mob guard ordered the other.

"What's in it? A special brand of booze?" asked the other guard.

"I don't know," answered the guard. "I just do what I'm told. And I'd suggest you do the same, and get a move on with that crate, if ya know what's good for ya."

The other guard placed his Tommy gun down to the side on the paved blacktop and walked up into the truck. Less than a minute had passed when he walked out carrying a crate with a large streak of black paint on the side. The guard patrolling the area waved him inside with the crate.

"I have to get inside and get to that crate without being seen," Cathal thought. He remembered studying many books on being covert and implementing close-quarters combat. He had thought this type of training was necessary to get in and out of this place without being noticed. The only problem was that he was wearing a long, hooded brown robe. He would generally wear this outfit where he came from—the Southern Uí Néill territory of Ireland in the tenth century. It was an outfit that didn't look anything like what the mobsters patrolling in and out of the warehouse were wearing. He needed to get in; he needed to blend in.

Cathal figured he didn't have much time before the boss got there, so he knew he had to act with haste. He studied the guard patrolling the back entrance. The guard kept walking back and forth in front of the wide loading dock and then disappeared around the corner for about thirty seconds.

That downtime was Cathal's only window of opportunity to get close enough to take him out.

As the guard vanished around the corner, Cathal looked in all directions, rapidly scouting the area to make sure it was safe enough to make his move. As it was, there was no one around now. This was his opportunity.

He dashed in a low crouching position toward the truck and slid under it just in time, before the guard turned the corner again. He lay there under the truck, watching the guard's every move for almost a minute. Out of the corner of his eye, he saw the Tommy gun not even five feet from his position—the same one the other guard had put down to transport the crate. He knew that this gun would help him to blend in as well as take out the other guard.

The guard rounded the corner again. Cathal quickly grabbed the Tommy gun and crouched next to the truck. Pressing his back against the truck, he prepared himself to take the guard by surprise. Cathal quickly studied the gun. He remembered reading about the Thompson submachine gun, a popular choice among the gangsters of the 1920s and the 1930s. He was a bit disappointed by this weapon's specifications after seeing other guns, such as the MP7A1, but he knew this world wouldn't develop those weapons for many years.

The sound of footsteps drew closer and closer toward Cathal. He clenched the gun tightly with his hands. He'd never used violence against another human being before. Ever since he was little, he'd had an extreme taste for adventure, always getting himself into danger wherever he could. He had an invincible attitude that drove his mother insane. As he got older, he spent a lot of time in the wilderness; he had become an adept in hunting. At the young age of twenty-three, he was already famous in his village for his lethal shot with a bow. People said that he never missed his mark, but this situation was something totally different: This guard in front of him wasn't just a helpless deer that couldn't fight back. His target now was a man, the top of the food chain—a man who was definitely more experienced in violence than him. If Cathal made one wrong move, it could mean the end for him.

Just as the guard came in range, Cathal sprang out and struck him in the head with the butt end of the gun, knocking him to the ground, unconscious. A sigh of relief rushed out of him. "Phew, that wasn't so bad. Now let's get you out of sight," Cathal whispered to the unconscious mobster. He cautiously dragged the body back to his previous hiding spot behind the car.

"You wouldn't mind if I borrowed some of your clothes for a little bit, would ya?" he jokingly asked the passed-out guard. "Didn't think so."

He began to take off the guard's pinstripe jacket, pants, and matching vest, slick black dress shoes, and white button-down shirt. He took off his own robes and put on the guard's well-kempt suit. Cathal wasn't too fond of the confined feeling brought on by these articles of clothing; he loved the looseness and warmth of his robes. He did, however, enjoy the smoothness of his new clothes. But he hardly had time to think about these miniscule things. He had a mission, and he needed to do it fast.

He rolled the limp guard underneath the car, leaving him with only his white undershirt, knee-length flannel drawers, and black knee-high socks. He spotted the guard's fedora lying on the pavement and decided he had better not leave it there. He picked it up and placed it on his head. He stared at his reflection in the window of the car and adjusted it with a downward tilt so as not to show his face completely. He wanted the perfect gangster disguise.

It was now time to infiltrate the warehouse and get to that crate. Cathal picked up the Tommy gun and hustled swiftly up to the side of the unguarded entrance and, with his back up against the old crumbling bricks, turned his head into the warehouse to evaluate the layout of the area. There were columns on each side, wooden crates stacked on top of one another. There were about four crates to each column, each of which measured ten to twelve feet high, he estimated. There were also aisles between the crates, where he could see armed henchmen moving to and fro.

"This is going to be harder than I had thought. There's no way I can keep track of all of them," Cathal muttered softly to himself as he looked up and saw even more guards on the second floor of the building.

For the next few moments, he studied the guards' patterns, and yet again, he found that most of them, like the previous guard, had a particular path that they patrolled. He was lucky to have these high columns of crates to block any view that the second-floor guards might have of him. He was also comforted by the fact that some of the guards were indulging themselves in the lovely booze that they were shipping in, thus leaving their judgment slightly impaired. "Shouldn't be partaking in their own product," Cathal thought. He wasn't happy that he couldn't see any sign of where the crate he needed was. There had to be some view of the don's office from another spot.

Cathal thought, "Why do I need to be so cautious?" He was, in fact, dressed as one of them. He felt divided. He didn't want to sneak by everyone, because that would make him look all the more suspicious. Still, he didn't want any of them to see his face and recognize him.

He tilted his fedora down even lower, walked into the building, and made his way around the outer right side. He didn't want to get caught up in the middle aisles between the crates. If he got caught in there, he could have guards swarm him from all sides.

He moved about cautiously. If he were found out, the odds would certainly be in favor of the mobsters—about twenty to one. Eventually, he made it to the front right corner. He peered around the stacked tower of crates and saw all the way to the back of the building. There was a lit-up room with glass windows and a door. Cathal assumed this must be the don's office, based on the descriptions he had read that said his office was a warehouse office.

He needed to make his move to the office now, and he needed to make it fast. Stealth and time were of the utmost importance to ensure his survival. Every moment wasted was another moment closer to the don making an appearance. He made his way toward the door at the end of the hall, stopping at every aisle to make sure no guards were close enough to make him as not one of their own. He passed eight rows of crates; the office kept getting closer.

His anticipation was running wild. Cathal had never done anything like this before. He stopped in his tracks just as a guard walked straight out into his path, not more than three feet in front of him, and then turned away from him. Cathal froze; his thoughts were in full chaos. He wasn't sure what to do, and if the guard had turned around, Cathal would surely have been caught.

Cathal gently placed the machine gun on the floor and did the only thing he could do. As fast as he could, he wrapped his left arm around the guard's neck, his biceps pressing against one side of the guard's neck, his forearm wrapped around the other side. He grabbed his right bicep with his left hand and used his right hand to press the guard's head down into his left arm. Squeezing with his left arm and pressing down with his right made this man's neck feel like it was being crushed in a vice.

The guard put up a little fight in the beginning, but soon enough, Cathal rendered him unconscious. He quietly lowered him to the floor and dragged him behind the crate. There was no way he could hide the body much better in there. Any one of the patrolling guards could see it from some angle. He had to get into that office, get the object, and get out before anyone saw this guard on the floor or, worse yet, saw him.

Picking up his gun, he made his way past the last two rows, carefully checking for guards. Then he entered the unlocked office. The office didn't look like it had seen much use. To his left was a large wooden desk. A brown leather bag with two handles leaned against it on the floor. On the other side of the office were two large filing cabinets, and to the left of them, resting on the tiled floor, was the crate with the large black streak along its side.

This was it. This was the crate with the object that he had left his normal everyday life for and traveled over a thousand years into the future to acquire. Cathal went up to the crate, placed the submachine gun on the ground, and used his hands to try to pry the crate open from the top. He tried as hard as he could to lift it up, but it wouldn't budge. It was nailed shut. He looked around the room to find something he could use to open it. A crowbar lay on top of the desk. Cathal picked it up and used it as a lever to prop up each corner of the crate, eventually loosening the top right off.

The crate was filled with straw. He pulled it out in clumps. Eventually, he uncovered one of the most magnificent things he had ever seen: a shiny black stone; an obsidian-colored God Stone. It was so shiny that he could see his own reflection—as if he was looking into a dark mirror. The shape of the stone was odd, as if it were one-quarter of a doughnut that had been cut into different pieces. The stone was about as long as his hand, but he needed both hands to hold it, for it was much heavier than any stone he had ever held of that size. Both sides of the stone had a symbol engraved onto it—four arrowheads staggered, representing mountains. "This must represent the earth power of the God Stones," Cathal whispered.

Cathal ran over and picked up the leather bag near the desk. He brought it back over to the crate. He picked up the stone, marveling at the craftsmanship of such work, and placed it in the bag.

"I guess the hard part is over," he said to himself. He got up with the bag, which was significantly heavier now. Cathal was making his way to the door to begin his clandestine escape, when he was met face to face with a puzzled guard.

CHAPTER TWO

"Who are you, and what are you doing in the don's office?" asked the henchman curiously. Clenching his Tommy gun tightly in his hands, the guard prepared himself to take Cathal down.

Cathal tensed up. His palms started to feel really clammy, wondering what he had gotten into this time. There was no stealthy exit or clever sneak attack. Cathal was going to have to use his wits to get out of this predicament. "I…um…the don told me specifically to come get his bag, the one you see here, and bring it to him first thing right when he arrived."

He made a poor attempt at presenting the leather bag in his hand.

"I didn't hear of any such order," the guard said. "I've got to be honest—I've never seen you before in my life. What's your name?"

"My name?" Cathal was trying to think of a name that could possibly help him get out of his current predicament. However, the guard noticed Cathal's hesitation and immediately knew something was wrong. He immediately lifted up his gun to knock Cathal in the head. In that brief moment, Cathal dropped the leather bag, which made a loud clanking sound as it hit the tiled floor. Without thinking, Cathal molded his free hand into a fist and struck the guard in the throat. Although the combative move was a smooth one, the strike left quite a mess. The guard pulled the trigger to his automatic gun as he fell backward, shooting bullets clear up into the brick wall. The bullets filled the chest of a guard patrolling the grated walkway directly above them, quickly bringing him to the ground in one abrupt thud.

The shots, which had echoed loudly through the warehouse, caused a commotion among the other patrolling guards, who started to run toward Cathal from all directions. Cathal quickly kicked the guard in the head, immobilizing him flat on the concrete ground. He then grabbed a grenade that fell out of the man's coat pocket, removed a handgun that was strapped to his waist, and picked up the leather bag.

This was not at all what he had hoped for. This incident was truly a test of his skills to get out of a dilemma easily. He couldn't believe this was happening so fast. Just the other day, he was hunting red deer along the outskirts of his village in Ireland, with not a worry in the world. Now he was a thousand years into the future and had an angry mob honing in on his position, ready to take him down without a moment's delay.

Cathal decided to use the path that he had already used to get to the office and turned toward the outer edges of the building, running past each aisle of crates. All he wanted was to get out alive fast, or he wouldn't be able to get out at all.

Cathal could hear a guard yelling different orders to the others: "We need to take care of this problem before the don gets here! He's running alongside the west walls! Take him down for questioning! Keep him alive!" He heard the clanking of footsteps stomping down the grated metal stairs and knew that his window of escaping was becoming narrower by the second.

When he was about halfway down the outer aisle, two guards popped out of nowhere, shouting to the other guards his location. They sprinted toward him, and after one fired a few rounds while running toward him, Cathal felt a sting on his left arm as one bullet clipped him there just below the shoulder.

Cathal grunted loudly and then made a sudden stop. He had never been shot before. Faltering with the pain, he fell to his knees for a moment but then stood up again, placing pressure on his arm with his other hand. Then he turned to the right and ran toward the center of the warehouse.

Within seconds, Cathal was spinning in midair. He slammed to the ground. With the wind knocked out of him, he saw stars in his vision and struggled in his effort to get onto his feet.

"You can stay right where you are if you want to live just a little bit longer!" shouted a guard, pressing the barrel of a gun to Cathal's forehead. The voice brought Cathal helplessly to his knees. The other remaining guards quickly sprang up from all directions, all pointing their guns at him.

Cathal began to feel light-headed. This type of pain was very new to him, and he was losing a substantial amount of blood. Still, he kept pressure on the wound with the other hand to cause as minimal blood loss as possible. He had read about how to apply pressure to wounds to slow down blood loss in that library about one hundred years into the future.

"Who sent you, and what are you doing here?" the guard demanded as he pressed the barrel harder into Cathal's forehead.

Cathal didn't know what to say. He was too busy assessing the situation and trying to figure out how he was going to get out of there alive. Besides this, there was also the fact that he continued to lose blood. He began to feel increasingly light-headed with every passing second. He located the leather bag on the ground, which was within an arm's reach. The guards had not noticed it yet, with all their attention exclusively focused on him.

"Who sent you?" the guard screamed at him. Another guard pressed down on Cathal's bullet wound with his gun. Cathal gave a yelp but remained impervious to the guard's questions and torturing tactics. His mind was racing with different scenarios that could result from different possible actions in this circumstance.

The main guard lifted his gun and shot off two rounds into the air. It was as friendly of a warning as he could have given Cathal. "Now, the next bullets that come out of this gun will be placed in your skull if you don't start to cooperate and answer our questions."

He knew that they weren't messing around any-more and that he would have to stall with some small talk until he could figure out what his next move was going to be. "I was...um...sent here to get informa-tion about your operation here and bring it back to my boss," stated Cathal, in an unsure way. He was hoping that the guards would supply him with some informa-tion, since he had forgotten to read about what fami-lies were competing with the Conti mob at this point in time.

"Which family are you from? The Capones? The De Lucia's?" the guard asked Cathal with a devious smirk.

"I can't tell you what family I'm from! They will kill me if I tell you!" pleaded Cathal, trying to sound sincere. He said this because he wanted to bide more time for his next move. A guard from behind ran up and stomped on his lower back, dropping Cathal to the floor.

"That's enough! Listen, boy. You will tell us what family you are with, or I'll kill you myself in a much more extensive, drawn-out, painful way than a bullet to the head," snarled the guard. He pushed Cathal back up to his knees and placed the gun to his head once more.

"I've got a note here in my pocket. I was supposed to hand it off to your boss," Cathal said as he remembered that he had taken a grenade off the guard he had knocked out earlier, and it just so happened to be in a spot that looked like it might have a note.

"Take it out slowly," the guard with the gun to his head said. Puzzled looks spread across all the guards' faces, while Cathal slowly slid his hand into his pocket and managed to pull the pin out of the grenade. He was not sure when it was going to go off, and his plan was to wait for the last possible second before it detonated.

From behind him, Cathal could hear cars pulling up, with people getting out and heading straight toward their very direction. "Ah, well, if it isn't the main man himself! We'll let him decide what to do with you!" The head guard started to laugh, and the others joined in simultaneously. Cathal knew he had run out of time. The don was here, and if Cathal didn't get rid of this grenade shortly, his whole body, as well as all the guards around him, would be spread out in pieces all over the floor and on the stacks of crates. But he had an immeasurable task to complete. If he failed, Cathal knew the whole world would plunge into darkness, and hell on earth would be inevitable as a result.

With the guards still laughing and enjoying the thought of Cathal's impending doom, he took the grenade out of his pocket and tossed it to his right, past one of the guards still laughing. He quickly reached for the leather bag and sprang up from his feet, as a loud bang came from the direction of the grenade. The explosion sent two guards flying toward the others. Wooden shards from the crates came whizzing by Cathal's head; one struck a guard in the neck, and he fell to the floor. He turned toward the exit, knocked two bewildered guards to the ground, and ran past.

Meanwhile, the explosions were spreading throughout the entire warehouse behind him, chasing him as he sprinted toward the exit. The guards who hadn't been taken out by the explosions were following right behind him, trying to escape as well, but they were becoming engulfed in the flames. One by one, each crate of liquor began to burst into flames, and the explosions convulsing from them sent flying debris of wood, hay, and glass in all directions.

He continued to rush to the open door in front of him, dodging various fragments of glass from the bottles and wood from the crates. As he ran, he saw two shocked guards run into the warehouse straight ahead of him. Cathal quickly pulled out his handgun and shot each of the guards twice in the chest.

He was almost at the exit, about seventy feet away, when a much shorter and rounder man came at him furiously, running directly toward Cathal. This man was dressed much nicer than the rest of the guards, which made Cathal guess that he was the don. If Cathal got by him, then he would be home free. He quickly pointed the gun at the don, whose right hand was clenched and surrounded by a glowing blue flame. He tried to fire two shots at him, but all he heard was two clicks. The gun had run out of bullets. As he got closer to the man, the blue flames engulfing his fist only became larger and larger.

The don whipped his flaming arm toward Cathal, hurling a ball of blue fire that came flying toward him with a loud shrieking sound. He ducked and dodged the blue flame as it soared past him and disappeared into the explosions. He kept running straight toward the confused don, shoved him to the side, and ran right out of the warehouse. From behind, he heard another shrieking sound, the same as before. He dove into a roll as another blue flame whizzed past his head.

He quickly slid behind the Lincoln Sedan from before to shield himself from any more attacks. He peered around the side of the vehicle toward the warehouse, which was now completely engulfed in flames. There was no sign of any mobsters. He suspected they must have all perished in that building.

Finally, Cathal began to calm down from this extremely stressful encounter. He wondered how he ever got involved in this whole situation, and he couldn't believe that he had only just begun this most epic and vital quest to secure the peaceful future of the world.

The dim sounds of police sirens grew louder and louder. He decided that it was time to get out of this place. Pressing down on his wound and clenching the leather bag, he looked down at the golden bracelet on his right arm. It shined brightly, reflecting the flames of the warehouse behind him. He closed his eyes and began to concentrate, whispering to himself, "Come on. Bring me back home. Bring me back home." With this, the bracelet began to glow a magnificent blue. His body began to shake, and the glow from the bracelet began to cover his entire body. In an instant, Cathal vanished into thin air along with the bag.

From a distance, on a nearby street corner, with a perfect view of where Cathal had been, stood a man, smirking. His clothing was not from the current period of time, but years into the future. He had on dark blue jeans and a hooded gray sweatshirt. The hood came over his face so much that you could only see the reflection of the flames in his eyes and an evil grin on his face. "Got you," he said to himself, and with that, he vanished into thin air just like Cathal had done—only with much more speed and ease.

CHAPTER THREE

Southern Uí Néill Region of Ireland—AD 947

Corncrakes scattered abruptly into the air, their rust-colored wings flapping vigorously as they disappeared into the midday murky sky. Fortunately for them, they were able to spot what the large red deer nearby could not. Cathal lay in the thick dewy grass of the rough meadow. He moved forward, dragging his body across the moist ground. He suspected that he was camouflaged from a distance, wearing earthy tones of brown and green.

Making sure not to disturb the large stag that seemed to be indulging in some long grass, he maneuvered his body carefully to rest on one knee. Cathal, who was larger than the average man, wasn't huge, but he had a strong muscular build. He had shaggy brown hair that almost reached his shoulders and a short, scruffy beard.

He reached out over his shoulder and pulled a long wooden arrow out of his quiver. The large stag stopped eating the grass and peered in his direction for a brief moment. Cathal held still, until it went back to eating from the ground.

Cathal lifted his *bogha*, a short wooden bow that he had made, with his left arm and nocked the arrow carefully in the center of his bowstring, allowing the shaft of the arrow to rest on the bow just above his grip. With his eyes staring intently on his target, Cathal raised his bow arm, kept his arm locked, and drew the string back until his thumb was resting against his jaw. Aiming at the stag one last time, he took a deep breath. His fingers became relaxed, letting the string slide through them. He heard the arrow whizzing through the air, and finally, he heard a thud.

The large deer moaned loudly and began to gallop, but after a few short strides, it fell over and went still. Cathal got up from his kneeling position and moved cautiously over to the injured animal. The deer had been lying on his side, hidden in the thick brush, twitching at a rate that decreased over time. An arrow stuck straight out of his neck, with a trail of blood running down toward the dirt. The deer's mouth was opening and closing very slowly, gasping for a couple of last breaths. Cathal, who wasn't fond of taking lives—even if they were animal lives—pulled out the arrow from the deer's neck and shot it once more to end its suffering. He hunted, not for sport, but for survival—to feed the ones he loved back home.

He placed a large sack on the ground, which he had over his shoulder, and pulled out a thick brown cloth blanket. He laid it out right next to the dead stag and rolled it over on top of the blanket. After he finished wrapping the deer in the cloth, he took a rope out from the sack and tied both ends tightly so the deer would be secure and wouldn't become unwrapped. He grabbed the remaining cloth and pulled it over his shoulder. He turned around and faced the direction of his village and began to walk into the fog, dragging the large deer behind him.

Cathal traveled at a fairly slow pace—for the deer was heavy and greatly hindered his speed—through thick meadows and light forests, until he finally reached the edge of his village. It was a few hours into the afternoon, and the village was rather lively.

The village had multiple homes with stone rock walls and roofs made up of straw and other various pieces of wood. Smoke rose above several huts into the sky. It was coming close to his evening mealtime. Finding a deer large enough to feed his appetite and mother's for several days was an all-day affair. He'd had to travel a good distance away from the village to get to their main feeding grounds.

As Cathal drew closer toward the village, he heard children laughing and yelling at each other. They spotted him dragging the large deer wrapped in cloth and started to hurry over to him.

"Cathal, what did you get this time? Did you bring us back some?" asked a young girl, in a joking manner. She was followed by two other boys, the same age, who seemed to agree with what she asked.

"Ha-ha, well, my young lady, if you would be so kind to grace us with your presence later, as well as with those of the two strapping young men beside you, I'm sure that I could spare some pieces!" Cathal responded enthusiastically.

"Will do. We'll stop by and nag you later tonight!" replied one of the boys, laughing, before they ran off to continue playing.

Cathal laughed and proceeded to walk once more into the heart of the village. There were men and women of all ages moving around outside their huts, hard at work. Some women were carrying heaps of clothing, some were milking cows, and some were cleaning in and around their houses. Many of the men were tending to their small farms or chopping wood to heat their houses as they prepared for the cold of night.

As Cathal walked by dragging the stag, men and women alike greeted him with waves and nods, while he returned their gestures. And then he stopped in his tracks, and his heart started to beat rapidly. A young beautiful girl, carrying recently washed clothing, walked toward him elegantly. Her long brown hair flowed with the wind, and her green eyes, which would leave any man in a trancelike state, caught his own. It was as if time had stopped all around, and she moved in slow motion.

Keela was her name. Her name meant beauty that only poetry could capture. Cathal didn't believe even that meaning gave her name justice. She and her father, Aidan, had moved to his village from the northwest when Cathal was just a young boy, about ten years ago. From the first day he had laid his eyes on her, Cathal knew that she was something special, and ever since then, they had secretly become the best of friends, and more. Aidan didn't approve of Cathal's lack of judgment with danger, hearing about all his adventures that would get him into trouble at such a young age. He didn't want that for Keela. But against his wishes, Cathal and Keela secretly found ways to see each other all the time. Cathal loved her very much, and she loved him back just the same. But for some reason, every time that Cathal laid his eyes upon her, it always seemed as if he had never seen something so beautiful and that he would immediately become rooted in his place.

Now, as she walked on by, she smiled and mouthed a "hello" in an adoring fashion. Cathal responded with the same greeting and turned his head to watch her beauty walk on by. She turned her head back to glance at him with a smile and then kept on walking. In public, they kept their relationship a secret to keep her father in the dark.

After the butterflies had left his stomach, Cathal continued on dragging the deer toward his hut. He walked by a couple more huts and smelled the aromas that signaled that it was getting closer to suppertime. His stomach started to growl from these smells, so he picked up his pace.

"Hello, my young lad! Looks like that poor deer wore you down!" shouted Crowley, an old man chopping wood.

"Ha! Nothing can evade my bow. You should know that by now, Crowley. I'm just feeling a little bit hungry. How are you doing?"

Crowley was dressed in old brown rags. He had short snow-white hair, with a scar over his left eye that kept it permanently closed. The scar started from his eyebrow and traveled down through his eye, ending halfway down his cheek. This scar always scared the children away from him, but for some reason, Cathal had always been intrigued by how he got it. Ever since he was a little boy, he would ask Crowley about it, and he would always tell him that there was a story behind his scar that he would tell Cathal when he got older.

"Well, well, I'm still not positive on the fact that nothing can evade your bow. But I will agree that you are a mighty fine shot." Crowley paused and smiled. "Well, you go on now and get something to eat. And don't forget about our meeting later tonight. Don't be late!"

"One day you'll believe me about my shot," said Cathal. "And don't worry—I'll be there on time."

He nodded to Crowley and continued to walk on by. Crowley was as much of a father figure to Cathal as one could be. Cathal couldn't remember his father. His mother always told him that he went off to war right after he was born and never returned. Crowley embraced him as his own and took up that role for him and for his mother. Other than helping them out, he stuck to himself. The village people were scared of him; mainly the scar on his face kept people away. Rumors would always flow through the village that he was crazy or that he was involved in dark magic. Cathal, being the adventurous one he always was, wasn't scared of this or what others would say but was fascinated by him.

Crowley didn't go back to chopping wood right away; he stared for a little bit at Cathal walking away. "The time has come. It must be tonight," he muttered under his breath. He looked over at the pile of wood he was chopping; then he focused on one piece. The piece started to shake and then hover above the ground. With his mind, Crowley maneuvered the piece of wood to float over to the chopping block. He picked up his ax and started to chop wood again.

Cathal made his way through the rest of the village until he arrived at his home, which was higher upon a small hill above the village. Smoke was rising into the air from the hut. His house was large enough for the two of them, one giant room to sleep and eat. His mother, Nora, was inside, preparing supper for the two of them. He placed the dead deer to the side of the wall outside his house and walked in.

"How was the hunt? Did the poor thing give you some problems?" asked his mother, who was cutting up vegetables and placing them in a stew that made Cathal's stomach ache more and more.

Nora was a strong woman. She practically raised Cathal on her own his entire life. She was grateful for Crowley's role in his life, as well. No matter what they did together to raise him, they couldn't keep his wandering mind from adventure. She always said Cathal reminded her of his father in that aspect, which ultimately led to his disappearance.

"No, no problem. He was a big fellow, though. Took me some time to drag him back here." As he answered, he sat down in a chair by the supper table and rested his head on the table face down.

"Don't get lazy on me, young man," his mother stated, continuing to cook. "You still have much more work to do today. I wasn't planning on you taking half the day to hunt for one deer. Food should be ready soon, and you still need to prepare the deer for later, as well as have your meeting with Crowley. Apparently, it is a very urgent matter that he has to discuss with you."

"I know, I know…I can't possibly imagine what he needs to talk to me about so urgently. He's had plenty of time to have this meeting with me in the past. He's practically my father...I guess I'll go outside and work on that deer until supper." Cathal got up from his seat and headed for the outside, dragging both feet in an apathetic manner.

After he finished preparing the deer for meals to come, Cathal went back inside to eat with his mother. "You know, Mother, I'm falling for someone. I'm falling in love with a girl in this village." He told his mother, thinking that the news would be a shock to her.

"Surely you must be talking about Keela?"

"Yes...How did you guess that so easily?" he questioned.

"Cathal, you've talked about her practically every day since the first day your eyes met hers. It's about time that you told me your true feelings for her. I can see why you are in love with her. She's beautiful and a wonderful person. And if you want to be with her, you must tell her!" Nora stated, while he gave a shocked, yet satisfied, look.

Cathal took a deep breath and nodded. "Yes, Mother, we do want to be with each other. We talk about it all the time. I'm just nervous about asking her hand in marriage...If I am so sure of how I feel, I suppose I should just ask her."

With that said, they finished up their meals and cleaned up after themselves. After they had done most of the cleaning, Cathal informed his mother that he was going to visit Keela for a little while.

A few minutes later, Cathal swiftly made his way down a main path in the village. The sun had just disappeared behind the trees along the mountainside, and the sky was beginning to darken with a red and orange glow. The walkway, which had once been loud with people talking and yelling, was now a much quieter, more desolate path. Many of the villagers had retired for the night or had gone inside for some relaxation.

As he neared Keela's home, Cathal abruptly slackened his pace. His speed abruptly slowed down once he reached her home. He cautiously made his way toward the door, which had been cracked open. There was a light illuminating the edges of the door from inside. As he peeked through the crack, he could see his desire standing with her back to him, cleaning near the fireplace.

Avoiding any sound, he pushed the door in slowly and moved toward her as if he were the predator and she were the prey. "Ah!" Cathal screamed as he quickly grabbed her.

Breathless from excitement, she pushed him away angrily and then pulled him closer to kiss him passionately. "How was your day, love?" Keela asked, smiling and staring into his eyes. "My father's been having me do chores all day, and I'm sick of them."

"Pretty good. Did you see the size of that deer I caught?" Cathal asked. "Where is Aidan? How much time do I have?"

She sighed and frowned. "He should be coming back any moment now. You must leave before he gets back, or he won't be too happy, and I'm sure I'll have to do more chores."

He agreed, in an uneasy way. "I know he doesn't like me being around you for some odd reason, but you and I are both twenty-three years of age. He should let you do what you want."

"Oh, I do wish I could express my feelings for you in front of him, but I wouldn't dare."

"Hmm, how about this?" Cathal held Keela's right hand with his and made her palm into a closed fist. Then he pulled up three of her fingers. "This will be our sign. It'll represent our love to each other, wherever we could possibly be."

"So the three fingers count for the three words in 'I love you'?" she asked as he nodded with a smile. "I like it. It's charming."

He smiled and sighed. "I should leave. I don't want to have you do more work because of me." He gave her a big kiss and turned away from her. He slowly headed for the doorway. They both held three fingers in the air as he disappeared.

After leaving her, he decided that it was now time to go see Crowley about this supposedly urgent meeting. He walked past a couple of houses on each side. By this time of night, everyone was in their homes with the doors shut. The orange and red glow of sunset in the sky was now gone, replaced with the night's darkness and bright stars. Cathal could not see a single person but himself walking around the village. The air had an eerie feeling, a feeling that had become more frequent as of late.

Cathal approached Crowley's hut and knocked on the door. Within seconds, the door creaked open; the old man with his mysterious scar stared out anxiously at him and then said, "Come in quickly, my dear boy. There is so much to tell, with such little time."

Crowley grabbed Cathal and vigorously pulled him inside and slammed the door.

CHAPTER FOUR

The inside of the hut was lit dimly. A large candle stood burning from the center of a small circular table. The table had two chairs around it. Crackling sounds came from a small fire that was burning in the background. Cathal walked over to one of the chairs and sat down.

"If there was ever a time that you really needed to listen to me and believe me, now is that time," Crowley warned him as he paced back and forth. Cathal smirked and gave a little chuckle, but then he became serious when he saw Crowley's stern reaction.

"Many, many years ago, there were godlike beings who ruled every aspect of this world," Crowley began. "They were the ones who made the mountains, rivers, deserts, and everything else on this wonderful earth that you can see, smell, hear, and taste. They were called the Greater Beings. These beings took our form to go about their everyday lives. They had our appearance and decided to create beings of much less power, ones who looked like them, to live and prosper on the lands that they had created. We are those beings. Everyone whom you know has come to be because of them. They made it possible."

"I always imagined there were such beings!" Cathal joked.

Crowley sneered. "Yes, there were such beings, and there still are such beings. Now if you will let me continue without your interruptions and jokes…" Crowley waited until he had stopped messing around. "There were two among the Greater Beings, who were much more powerful than the rest—Viktor and Terranos. Viktor was extremely virtuous, a true leader of might and courage. He believed in peace and had a strong, caring desire for all living things. Terranos was as powerful as he was great. However, he was very mischievous in his ways. He sought power most of all and hated any human who didn't worship him."

"I've overheard songs of the great Viktor and Terranos," said Cathal, now more serious. "I have heard you sing them when you worked outside around the house. What did they look like?"

"Oh, so you pay attention to my songs. Well, Viktor was grand in stature, taller than anyone you've ever seen in your life. He was very muscular and had long, golden blond hair, with a thick beard. He wielded a sword that was as long as he was tall, and the blade was as wide as your head. There were songs that described his armor that glistened so bright with gold that you could see him from faraway distances, and some even mistook him for the sun."

Crowley walked over to the cauldron hanging over the fire and stirred the contents within it. "It was said that if any humans gazed upon Terranos, either they would have nightmares for every fourth night for the rest of their lives, or they would worship him forever to the utmost. He stood about a head taller than Viktor, towering over the rest of the Greater Beings. His armor was darker than the night and hotter than fire. They say that most, if not all, weapons that came in contact with it melted. Viktor's sword was one of the only known exceptions to this rule and could melt it easily. Terranos wore a black cloak with a hood that darkened his face so that you could only see his bright red eyes. And he wielded a flail that had a long chain, which held a spiked club as large as a man's chest."

"This Terranos fellow, he sounds pretty intense. I couldn't imagine swinging a club of that size. And Viktor sounds like the total opposite but equally as strong."

"That they were. Everything that Viktor loved and appreciated, Terranos hated and despised. Their powers were both very evenly matched, but in the end,

Terranos's inability to control his emotions and powers led to his defeat."

Crowley grabbed two bowls, scooped out the stew he was cooking in the cauldron, and poured them into the bowls. He walked over, sat down next to Cathal, and handed him one of them.

"Thanks." Cathal took a sip and looked pleased. "You always were a good cook. So what happened next? You said Terranos's powers and emotions led to his defeat. What happened? Was there a battle?"

"Indeed there was, my young man. And a great battle it was. In fact, it was a battle of the ages. There has never been a battle of such magnitude, and I hope, for this world's sake, that there isn't one ever in the future."

The fire cracked in the background. It kept the inside of his hut extremely comfortable. His fires were always the best compared to everyone else's hut, which would go out or would never be warm enough.

Crowley took a couple of sips from his bowl and continued. "Terranos desired power above all else and became obsessed with ruling over all the Greater Beings. There were events that took place that I can't get into at this point in time that Terranos caused, but these events concluded with a separation of the Greater Beings. Half of them joined Terranos, and they became known as the Tarnok. The other half followed Viktor, and they became known as the Elluna. Terranos convinced the Tarnok that Viktor was planning to take all the power away from the rest and rule supremely over them all. However, little did they know that this was actually Terranos's very own intention. And so the Great War began, an epic battle between the Tarnok and the Elluna."

"Were there also humans involved in the war?" Cathal asked. His full attention was now fixated on Crowley's tale.

"Yes, there were. There were human followers who were very close to the Greater Beings before the split between the Tarnok and the Elluna. They consisted of humans from all over the world, of different backgrounds and cultures. They were the humans who had ruled the lands by historical record. The Greater Beings gave them this privilege. However, they told them what to do. There were humans who worshipped and shared the beliefs of the Tarnok, and there were also humans who had done the same toward the Elluna. These different groups of humans had problems between each other, even before the split, so that the Greater Beings would end up resolving these conflicts. When the split happened, so did the humans who worshipped them. Either they joined the side of the Tarnok and became known as the Tarnen or they joined the side of the Elluna and became known as Elluna's Guard.

"Elluna's Guard and the Tarnen also had battles against each other throughout the world and throughout time. These battles were known throughout history very publicly. However, only a select few in these clans knew what the battles were truly about. Many of the humans fighting for the Tarnen and Elluna's Guard believed they were purely fighting for territory or religion and not for the Tarnok or the Elluna. They were sorely mistaken. They were puppets in a scheme much grander than they could fathom."

"Crowley, this story is very interesting, and I'm glad that you're telling me all this," Cathal interjected. "But what does this have to do with me, and why is it so urgent that you have to tell me this now?"

Crowley smiled as he took away the bowls and placed them in a tub of water. "This has everything to do with you. You will become part of the stories that I am telling. Only you haven't determined the course of those tales yet."

Confusion and frustration rushed through Cathal. "You aren't making any sense to me, Crowley. How am I supposed to be a part of these stories? I haven't done anything remotely of great importance. People in this village have been telling me that you have been becoming a little on the crazy side, and I was denying it until now, but I think that they're right."

"Let me continue, and you will see that I am not crazy, and that this is very real." Crowley chuckled as he said this. "I could care less of what the folks in the village are saying about me, you know that."

Crowley walked back over to the empty chair and sat down.

"The Greater Beings' power is their life force," he continued, after a little while. "The more power they use to create extraordinary things or to use magic, the more they drain their life away from themselves. The power does slowly come back over time. However, the more power they use in a short period of time, the closer they are to death."

"So what you are telling me is that when the Greater Beings create trees or mountains, they could use up too much power, and this slowly kills them? And if they stop using their power for a period of time, their powers would regenerate."

"In a way, yes. That is correct. And thus, when the Elluna and the Tarnok went to war, they used an abundance of their powers. What a great war it was, Cathal! It spanned grand distances and destroyed many beautiful cities. The land where this war took place on, the land they once called home, became an enormous, desolate desert, stretching in every direction. In the end, both sides were worn down to the nigh brink of death, but the Elluna salvaged the powers they had left and combined them in one final attempt to win the war—they created a blast of light that shot the Tarnok off into the far reaches of the stars. It was said that, in that moment, the blast engulfed the whole world in a light brighter than the sun above. The Elluna and their human followers had won the war and restored order to the lands. The Tarnen, who were without their masters, retreated to the corners of the earth."

"Wow, I would have loved to have seen the Tarnok blasted away like that," said Cathal. "That must have been a huge victory for the Elluna. Getting rid of the Tarnok would definitely restore peace."

Cathal got up from his chair and began to head for the door to leave. "Thanks for the great story. I'll come back another time so you can finish it."

"Sit down, Cathal!" Crowley demanded as he stood up from his seat. "I've only just begun to tell you what you need to know. Now I will tell you how you are involved in all this."

Cathal's face was now finally aroused with curiosity, and he walked back over to the chair again to sit down. "You've got my attention now."

Crowley sat back down and began to speak once more. "The blast didn't destroy the Tarnok—it only shot them out to the far reaches of the stars. For the earth's protection, the Elluna used more of their powers to create beings that patrolled the skies far beyond, to warn them if the Tarnok were to ever return. They were called the Outer Rim Guard, and if they were to ever spot the Tarnok, their number one priority was to send one back here to warn the Elluna. You see them every night when you look up into the sky. Many resemble the stars that you see twinkle in the night. When you see a star shoot across the sky, it is probably one of the Outer Rim Guards moving at speeds unimaginable."

Cathal now had a surprised look on his face, but he remained speechless.

"The war took a huge toll on the Elluna, and they were exhausted from using their powers. They wanted to live as normal a life as possible from that day forth. They all wanted to have a minimal amount of powers, because the war drained them to the brink of death. So they all agreed to place the majority of their powers into a group of stones. These stones, when joined together, form a disklike shape. They are known as the God Stones. Each stone represents a different power. Viktor has the core power that holds them all together. Along the outside, wrapped around the stone, Viktor stored the powers of earth, water, fire, and sky. In total, there were five magical stones that held the power for this world's creation and survival. They did this so that if one day the Tarnok came back, they could retrieve their powers to defend this world from tyranny once again. Viktor entrusted the God Stones to Elluna's Guard. Hence, their name is associated with guardianship. He told them to keep them safe and to hide the stones until the day when the Tarnok would return, if it ever were to come to pass."

Crowley stood up and began to pace around the room, agitated. "With most of their powers gone, the Elluna slowly blended into human society, living the lives of normal humans. Some of them were heard of on a rare occasion. It is said that Viktor later went into hiding and secretly became a member of Elluna's Guard without them knowing, to use his knowledge to help and aid them. Throughout hundreds of years, the Tarnen and Elluna's Guard have fought many battles, tales of which you have heard throughout history. And one day, a terrible tragedy took place—the Tarnen succeeded in stealing all the God Stones."

"You mean they stole the powers of the Elluna, which would be needed to save the world if the Tarnok were to ever come back?" Cathal asked.

Crowley nodded. "The Tarnen knew the great importance these stones had to the Elluna, so they spread them out all throughout the world in secrecy, making it absolutely impossible for Elluna's Guard to retrieve them. If the Tarnok were to come back, the Elluna would be helpless without them, and the world would meet its inevitable doom and would be in utter chaos and death. Anyone who didn't worship Terranos and the Tarnok would become their slaves. Men, women, and even children would live the rest of their lives in misery, and even this fate would prove lucky for them."

Crowley walked over to some blankets and pulled them off. Revealing a wooden chest, he began to fiddle with a lock. "Angered by this theft, Viktor used some of his powers to look into the future and saw that the Tarnok would come back to earth to cause utter mayhem. And he also saw that they will be unstoppable unless the stones are retrieved. He was able to find out when the Tarnok would arrive back on earth, and he wrote down the date he discovered. He also looked into the future and was able to see when the Tarnen would be hiding each of the stones at their most vulnerable moments. He saw that it was neither he nor any of the other Elluna, who would be able to steal these most precious stones back. It would have to be one of human blood. Viktor also saw that this human would also have to be one who possessed the same qualities that he himself had—bravery, stealth, and might. In order to help this young man, Viktor wrote down on a scroll all the dates when these opportunities for retrieving the stones were paramount."

Crowley opened the chest and took out an object, a scroll, which he placed on the table. Cathal began to reach for it. "Not yet," said Crowley. "There is more for me to explain. Now these dates Viktor pinpointed were spread throughout history during times of great anguish, which were all directly linked to the Tarnen. He saw that it had to be the same human to take back all that which was stolen."

Crowley walked back over to the chest and began sifting through it again. "The only problem was that some of these dates were hundreds of years apart. How would a mere human be able to get to all these dates in his lifetime? Viktor needed a way for that person to get to all these dates. He needed that person to travel through time. So with some of the powers that he still had, he forged a golden bracelet and filled it with the power of time travel. And he made sure that whoever wore it would be able to travel through time and go to whatever location he or she desired."

Crowley took out another object from the chest and placed it on the table next to the scroll.

Cathal's eyes widened in wonderment and awe. The bracelet shined so bright, reflecting everything around it. Dark blue diamonds were embedded around the bracelet in such a way that it looked as if no one had forged the bracelet at all; it was as if it came into being naturally.

"This, Cathal, is where you come into this tale. Viktor was able to see that the man he needed to carry out this most dangerous quest was of Irish blood. He also foretold that the date that this man would accept this quest is today. I was given the great honor of protecting these items with utmost secrecy until this day, to find out who would be the one. And I believe this man to be you, Cathal. You have all the qualities that Viktor has foreseen. I am sure it is most certainly you."

Cathal stared at the two mysterious objects lying on the table next to him. It was almost as if they were calling out to him. He became more spellbound every second. He swallowed hard and began to speak. "I don't understand. There's no way that I could conceivably be that person. There's so many other people more suited for the task at hand. And I don't even believe that this bracelet could actually make you travel through time."

"There can be no one else!" Crowley shouted in a demanding tone. Then he decided to soften his voice once again. "Cathal, I've known you since you were born. I've cared for you as if you were one of my own. I love you dearly and wouldn't be presenting you with this quest if I had a choice in the matter. However, I don't have a choice, and you are the one who will bring this story to an end, an ending of light, free of darkness."

"Even if I am who you say I am, the one who is supposed to take back the God Stones, I don't believe that one can simply travel through time. I'm also deeply in love with Keela. I want to have a family with her one day—soon if I can—and if I do this quest, and it is all true what you've said, I fear I shall not return."

"Cathal, this is very real, and I'm afraid to say it, but you have no choice in the matter. You now have a greater responsibility to this world than anyone has ever had, god or human alike. If you don't accept this quest and fulfill it, then everyone you love and the whole world will meet an end worse than death itself. You must see this out until the end."

"How does this affect us if they don't come back for another couple hundred years? I mean, I will be long gone by the time this happens anyway. Why should I worry about this? Why should I risk my life? Why do I have to just stop my life?" Frustration boiled out of Cathal, as questions spewed from his mouth.

"The Tarnen know about such a man who will try to take back the stones. They don't know when he will strike, but they do know where he is from and when he is living. I'm sure they will be sending someone after you and your loved ones soon. We have to act with extreme haste."

Cathal stared off blankly into the fire and slowly started to nod his head. "I could never accept the thought of having the ones I love come to such a dreadful end if I had the chance to do right by it, no matter how dangerous it could be. All right, I accept. But I do not know what I need to do or where I need to go on these dates, let alone how to use this bracelet."

"Thank you, Cathal. The world shall never truly understand how much your actions will save their lives. I will teach you what you need to know and guide you along this perilous journey. Only you have the will and power to see this through to the end. You must be extremely cautious—straying but a little could end any chance of saving everything you hold dear."

CHAPTER FIVE

Cathal stared intently at the mysterious objects that were placed on the table before him. "If this 'end of the world' story is really true, and if I have to travel to all these different places throughout time and save the world, as you put it, there must be an extraordinary amount of things I must know in order to go through with it all."

"Correct. And I shall go over all these concerns with you now." Crowley abruptly began to cough, but then he regained control. "It appears that my age is catching up with me, Cathal. Nevertheless, this is what you need to know—once your body has lived in a certain time, you can't go back to that specific time. It is impossible for there to be any instantaneous time where your body is in two places at once. This means that you can't relive anything you have already lived."

A disturbed look fell over Cathal's face. "So if I wanted to go back and do something over that I have already done, there is no possible way this could happen—because my body has already lived in that time?"

"Unfortunately, I would have to say no to anything like that happening. You cannot change what you have already done. Because of this issue, you have to be very careful when you do anything. For you will not be able to do it over. There are no second chances. I'm afraid to say that if you fail to recover any of the missing stones, there may be no way of getting another chance. The Tarnen did an exceptional job at hiding the stones. The dates Viktor picked are very small windows of time, and you must do everything right the first time."

Cathal laughed to cover up the uneasy feeling flowing through his body. "Crowley, you're telling me that if I fail only once at any one of these moments, this whole quest might as well not even begun? You're not leaving me much room for faults."

Crowley nodded with a sense of pity. "This means that every single action you take is of the utmost importance. You can't tell any living soul about what is going on, not even those who are most dear to you. If the wrong person finds out, this information could possibly change the history of mankind and ruin your chances. There are only two people who know of this quest you are going to take, and that is you and I."

"Can't I tell even Keela?"

"If one person finds out who shouldn't, those dates could become useless. The Tarnen might spread word of this and cause a movement of the stones that wasn't foreseen. No one else can know. After you take back each of these stones, you will need to have a place where you know they will be safe. I would suggest somewhere here so that you can gather them all together and know exactly where they are when the time comes."

"Can this be somewhere in the village?"

"No, that is too close to someone beyond the two of us. You need to find a place that is very secluded to all living people. I would suggest somewhere far away, deep in the forest."

Cathal's eyes gazed into the fire. So many thoughts were racing through his head. He wondered how on earth he would be able to do this on his own. Crowley was much too old to come along with him. As for him, well, all he could really do was hunt with a bow and use a sword. Was that really going to help him against armies of men?

Crowley snapped at Cathal to regain his attention. "I must warn you—the times that you will be adventuring to span hundreds of years. Many generations will have come and gone, creating many new things, some good and some bad. Each one of these places you will go to shall be very different. You will need to know everything there is to know in the world to help you succeed—hundreds of years of knowledge."

"And how do you suppose I can learn hundreds of years of knowledge?" asked Cathal. This idea deeply concerned him.

"Stand up, Cathal." Crowley walked over to him as Cathal rose from his chair. Cathal attempted to speak, but before he could do so, Crowley placed his palm on his forehead, and he warped into a trancelike state. A bright white light began to shine from Crowley's forehead. The light traveled down his face, through his arm, and down his hand, and as it reached Cathal's head, it vanished. Cathal's body began to shake, and his feet lifted off the ground and hovered a few inches above floor. This happened for a matter of seconds, and then with his body still, his feet returned to the ground.

Cathal snapped out of the trance and opened his eyes in amazement. "What just happened to me? When you touched my head, I felt an amazing jolt rush through my body." Cathal waved his arms and legs around as if he felt he were using them for the first time.

"Since we have very little time, I have just passed some powers from myself to you. These powers will allow you to read and learn things at tremendous speeds."

Cathal anxiously interrupted Crowley. "So you really can create magic. There's always been talk through the village that you were different from everyone else. Now I know why. I do have a question, though—why do we have very little time? I mean if I can travel through time, shouldn't I have all the time in the world?"

"I feel the presence of some unknown evil lurking over this land and over our actions in the near future. I don't know how much time we shall have before this happens. We must do all we can now to try to prevent this."

"So you are telling me that the actions I do in other times can possibly help prevent these evils from happening?"

"In a matter of speaking, yes. But we cannot dwell over what we do not know. What we do know is that you must get prepared for the task at hand. Now as I was saying before I was interrupted. Since you will be all over the world at different times, you will need to know different forms of communication, different native tongues of those places you visit. I have passed on that knowledge to communicate in every single form as well."

"I will be able to speak in every language?" Cathal's eyes widened.

"Yes, you will hear what they have to say, but the words coming out of their mouths shall be of your own tongue to you. And you will talk back to them the same way, but they will hear their language."

Crowley picked up the bracelet and began to pace around the room, stroking the shiny wonder. "The world, as you know it, is minuscule in size. It is far larger than you could possibly imagine. Years from now, explorers will reach a new world, an undiscovered land. You shall read all about this once you set forth on your quest."

"How do you know all this, Crowley? You keep surprising me with knowledge that no one should know."

"These aren't stories, my dear boy. This is real. I have been around a long time, and I have seen many things. Right now I can't tell you how I know all this. There will come a time when I can share this with you. But I fear that this information, if you know any more, may endanger what we are trying to accomplish at this time. Now, getting back to reading these books—in order to find out more about these special dates and what is going on during these times, you must read as many books on these matters as possible."

As Crowley continued to speak, Cathal began to zone out again. When he had started the day this morning, he could never have imagined that this meeting would have taken a turn like this. He really had no idea what Crowley was talking about in general until Crowley had touched his head. Within that moment, everything that he had been talking about had become quite clear.

"Are you paying attention?" asked Crowley. "This is rather important to your survival. Before you start going to these certain dates in time, you must go to a time a little before the final date. You must go to a library where thousands of books are held. You must read all the information on everything that has happened in the world to help you on these missions. Having this knowledge will give you an advantage to your foes. You will also need to use this information to figure out where to go for all these dates. Reading these books will help you make this decision. Besides reading books about what has gone on in the world, you must read about other things to help you with survival—combat, hand to hand, as well as weapons and stealth."

"Have you seen me with a bow and sword lately? I'm pretty sure that I don't need help in that area."

Crowley laughed harder and harder, a fit that ended with a cough clearing his throat. "Cathal, over time, the world changes drastically. Man creates new weapons all the time, ones much more powerful than we have, weapons that can kill hundreds of thousands of people at one time in a single instant."

Cathal was shocked by all this information, but after all that he had heard, he didn't question him on the validity of any matter being discussed. "All right, I see where you are going with this, but are you really expecting me to read every single page of every book?"

"Not necessarily. I've passed on to you some unique abilities. One of these abilities involves these books. All you have to do is find a book you want to read, hold on to it, and clear your mind of everything but that book. If you focus hard enough, all the information within those pages will become a part of you. You will know everything in that book. You will be able to do everything the book talks about. You will be able to know the tastes, smells, and visuals being described in that particular book. If you are unsure of this, just wait and try it out for yourself. It is quite fun to go through with this process."

"So if this whole thing with the books is possible, how will I be able to time travel to the right times and places using that bracelet?"

"Ah, the mystery behind this magnificent piece of jewelry." With care, Crowley placed the bracelet back onto the table near Cathal. "When Viktor was in the early stages of forging the bracelet, he looked throughout time and saw how the world was during these dates, and he was able to embed them within the bracelet. So all the wearer has to do is to think of that place and of the contents of what was going on during that time, and the bracelet could tell where and when to take the wearer. The bracelet acclimates to the one who wears it."

Cathal gently picked up the bracelet and stared deeply into the dark blue crystals embedded around the radiant gold. Cathal matched the size of the bracelet with his arm. He thought it was more like an arm guard covering half of his forearm, but he wasn't going to question Crowley on what it should be called. He couldn't stop pondering how something as simple as this bracelet could possibly have the power that Crowley said it had.

"Believe it, Cathal. You must believe in its powers for it to work. Viktor was very wise and very skilled. One of these skills was being able to accommodate humans. He took a great fascination in the human thought and needs. With this knowledge, he was able to prepare this bracelet to work accordingly."

Confidence began to build within Cathal, and he finally began to believe in Crowley and in what he had to do. He took a deep breath and nodded to Crowley, letting him know he was ready for what was ahead. "I believe I should be on my way to this library to gather all the knowledge that I can." Cathal grabbed the bracelet and the scroll and placed them in the satchel he had brought with him. They walked toward each other and hugged. Crowley held him tight, like a father holding his son, knowing that he might never see him again. Cathal nodded good-bye to Crowley. He didn't know what to say, so he headed for the door.

"Wait! Let me go over once more on what you must do." Crowley began to emphasize the importance of several aspects of Cathal's quest. "It is of great importance to do everything correctly. You cannot relive any moment that you have already lived. It is impossible for there to be any moment where you are in two places at once. This means that every action you take must be taken with great care. If you fail even one thing, it could change history and, even worse, ruin our chances of saving this world. You can't tell anyone else about this—knowledge of this could jeopardize their lives and everyone else's. Don't ever bring items from different time periods to other times to help aid you—this could change history as well. You can come back here when you need aid from me and when you want to hide the stones. But make sure that whenever you use that bracelet, no one sees you. You must find a place here where you can hide the stone pieces as you acquire them. It must be somewhere secluded, away from the village. And, finally, when you are searching for the God Stones, their locations should stick out. They could possibly be in special areas, which are much more guarded than the others."

Cathal took in his words again, but his thoughts were gray in one area. "You say that I can't go back to times I've lived in because it is impossible for my body to be in two places at once. But how am I going to be able to bring the stones back if they also are in two different places at one time? I mean, as we speak, the Tarnen have them held somewhere. How can I bring that stone back and have that same piece somewhere else at the same time?"

"These stones have special powers, and they are an exception to the rule. Because all the possible moments to take the pieces are in the future, it does not affect the pieces right now during this time. When you retrieve them, they will cease to exist in that time and any time forward because you would have brought them back here."

Waiting for him to understand, Crowley stared at Cathal, and Cathal returned the stare with a look of agreement. "Now the first place you go should be a library around the year 2013. If you think of a library in 2013, the bracelet will take you to one. I will give you a hint on the first date on the scroll. This is the only one

I know of for certain. It is on May 23, 1924, Chicago, Illinois, United States. It is during the Prohibition, involving a mob family." Cathal's puzzled look covered his face once again, and Crowley laughed as he said, "Hah! Don't worry, you'll learn all about it."

Crowley gave him a stern final warning. "And, finally, be safe. This will be extremely dangerous. And in the end, if you succeed, you will have experienced things far more evil and dangerous than any human has ever encountered. I fear there are things of immense evil out there, and they will stop at nothing to see you fail. This journey is a long one, one that is unfortunately filled with danger and sorrow, but there is a glorious light at the end. If you reach that end, it will be the greatest victory the world has ever known or not known at all. You will be an unsung hero."

And with that, Cathal vanished out the door. Crowley, alone, fell into a chair. "I hope, for the world's sake, that this was the right thing to do. I wish you well, my boy."

Nervously, Cathal continued to walk away from Crowley's hut. This meeting with Crowley had forever changed his life. His life wasn't ever going to be the same. The normal life of deer hunting and sneaking around with Keela was over. He had to save the world.

As night fell, all Cathal could hear was his very own footsteps as he made his way through the village. He couldn't stop thinking about Crowley's last words. What did Crowley mean about evil forces out there trying to stop him? The only things that he had ever encountered were deer and the occasional wild animal that would try to attack him when he would go on one of his adventures against his mother's wishes. These animals were harmless creatures compared to the perils that Crowley had described. Every now and then, he would have a minor scuffle between other boys in the village, but none of it was serious. But the idea of evil forces out there that would stop at nothing to kill him frightened him, and it made him want to throw up. He actually did this in some bushes not far from Crowley's hut.

Once he was finished throwing up, he made his way to Keela's home. He peered through a window and watched her sleep. She was as beautiful as an angel, and he longed to hold her. The sight of her made him want to stay and never go on this journey. There was absolutely nothing he would change about her. To him, she was perfect in every single way. But it also inspired him to do well for her, his love. He placed three fingers on the windowsill and whispered, "I will be back for you. I love you." He decided he could no longer linger. He moved on.

He made his way toward his own home. He cracked the door open to see his mother, who was also sound asleep, and he whispered to her, "I will make you proud." Then he continued toward the forest that covered the mountainside. At the forest edge, he glanced back at the village he'd been raised in ever since he could remember. He wondered if this would be the last time he would see it. He took in a large breath of air and turned around to enter the forest.

He walked deeper and deeper through the woods and up the mountainside. He had walked for a couple hours when he found the spot where he decided he would hide the God Stones. The sun began to creep above the mountain. There was a small cave that formed underneath an enormous tree. It was large enough for a man to crawl in and hide, but there was room for nothing else.

Cathal sat down beside the tree and took out the bracelet. The diamonds shined bright in all directions. The gold reflected his figure as if it were studying him. It began to vibrate in his hands as he held it, and then it slowly stopped. He stared deeply into the dark blue diamonds as if there was no end to them. In frustration, he placed it on the grass next to him. "What if Crowley wasn't messing with me, and this is real?" he asked himself. "What if I never see my friends and family again? What if I never see Keela again? What evils are out there waiting for me?"

With all these questions racing through his head, his stomach began to churn again. He quickly turned his head away from the bracelet and threw up once more on the ground behind him. After he had finished, he pulled himself together and placed the bracelet on his right wrist. It clung to him immediately as if it was molded to his forearm.

He grabbed the satchel with the scroll and began to stare at his bracelet, which now felt as if it were one with his arm. He stared deeply at his own gold reflection and then into the blue diamonds. He thought long and hard about the destination Crowley had told him: "Library 2013, library 2013, library 2013." Light began to emit from the bracelet; it became greater and greater, but then it faded. Frustration overwhelmed him. He lay down and closed his eyes for several minutes to rest and collect his thoughts.

Eventually, he became completely relaxed. He cleared his mind and thought of nothing but a library and the year 2013. A light started to emit from the bracelet again. This time it began to cover his arm and then his upper body; eventually, his whole body was glowing a bright blue color. His body began to tremble as wind swirled around him. Leaves ripped from their branches and encircled him. Trees swayed back and forth. He began to scream with pain, and within an instant, he vanished. The wind calmed down. The leaves fell to the ground, and the trees came to a rest. Cathal was no longer in tenth-century Ireland.

CHAPTER SIX

Newark, Delaware—April 25, 2013

The night air was crisp and calm. College students laughed and conversed as they walked to and from various university buildings. A small gust of wind picked up on a street corner. The street signs began to rattle; traffic lights swayed from side to side. A bright light formed in the yard on the corner of two intersecting roads. The light got larger and brighter. *Crack!* The light disappeared, and in its place was a confused man, clothed in brown robes. Cathal, astonished the time travel bracelet had actually worked, fell to the ground. Now with his satchel in hand, he peered through the bushes at his surroundings.

Large buildings surrounded him in every direction. He thought they might be castles, different from his own time, but they didn't seem equipped for any type of siege. He saw what looked like large trees, but there were no branches or leaves coming off them—only bright lights that hung from the tops. They were similar to torches, but they weren't made of fire. He saw other lights that were hanging from the air, with their different colors switching between green, yellow, and red. He was already amazed by this time period. "What type of wizardry is this?" he asked himself.

He crawled past the grass he was lying on and onto a hard gray surface, much like the stone walls of his home but smoother. They looked like paths to him; however, the paths of his village were of dirt, but these were of a hard stonelike surface, shaped perfectly. Cathal stood up to get a better look at his surroundings. There were much larger paths farther away than the one he was standing on, large black paths with yellow and white lines painted on them. There were many noises and rumblings he was unfamiliar with. He looked up and saw a sign that said S. College Ave. He suspected this must be the path he was on. Still shocked that he could understand what the sign meant, he looked around for other signs, one that might lead him to a library.

After scanning the area for several moments, he saw a sign that said Morris Library. With excitement, he ran across the large black pathway, looking only at the sign.

Beep!

"Watch it, freak!" a pissed-off driver screamed as two bright lights swerved by Cathal, making him fall to the blacktop of the road.

"What was that?" he asked himself. Never in his wildest dreams did he think people would be transported by anything but boat and horse. Cathal stood up and brushed himself off. He heard chuckling from a distance.

"Look what that guy is wearing," a boy said to a girl walking with him. They both giggled and kept moving.

"Look at what you all are wearing, ha!" Cathal yelled back at them as they continued to giggle, walking down the pathway. Cathal thought their clothing attire was rather strange. The boy was wearing baggy Nike mesh gym shorts and a dark blue University of Delaware Blue Hens hoodie, while the girl had on a blue jean skirt with a white jacket. He continued to walk toward the library on a brick pathway with beautiful well-kept bushes on both sides. Buildings surrounded him in every direction he looked, and they were all of the kind he surely wasn't used to. Peering at the side of the library, he saw large openings high above with people. They seemed to be focused very intently on various things. The lighting inside the building amazed him.

Cathal reached the front of the building and made his way up the concrete steps before him to the front entrance of his destination, Morris Library. He saw two large openings into the building. He walked up to them and saw a metal bar going horizontally across the middle of the opening. He crouched down and attempted to go underneath the bar. *Bang!* He smashed his head into the glass door. He was immediately knocked backward. The pain in his head caused a slight amount of dizziness. Confused by what just took place, he stood up and cautiously walked back to the door and pressed his hand up to the glass. He moved his hands all over the glass, trying to figure out how to open the door and get past it.

Giggling from behind, a small girl came up and pulled the door open. She waited momentarily, holding the door open for him with a smile on her face. "Here ya go," she said.

Smiling back, Cathal bowed and walked through, saying, "Thank you, my lady." He followed her to the next set of doors and mimicked the way she had opened the previous set. "My lady," he said again. She smiled, thanked him, and continued through.

He found it very strange that this language he was speaking and understanding was similar but also very different from his own. He had no idea how Crowley made it so that he could understand everything they said and how his responses back were intelligible. Cathal continued to walk further through the building past the main lobby.

In front of him, he saw a man standing behind a tall table, focused on a black rectangular device, which sat on top of the table.

"May I help you, sir?" the man stated, still staring at the black device in front of him. He looked at Cathal and smirked.

"Can you tell me where I can find books on history, please?" The question sounded scripted as it came out of his mouth, as though he had been practicing the line awhile.

The man giggled a little, and his eyes rolled back for a brief moment. He smiled as if his coworkers were playing a joke on him. "Follow me, sir," he said, motioning Cathal to follow.

They made their way walking past several tables and up some stairs. The large room they entered was filled with tables and people sitting at them, quietly reading from books spread out on their tables. Many were quietly pressing their fingers down vigorously on smaller glowing devices.

He was not used to such a quiet place. The only sounds he could hear were their own footsteps, and the light clicks coming from the people pressing down on those glowing devices.

The worker brought Cathal to a place deep into the library with books all around. Row after row of endless books was there. "Well, here is the start of the history section," the man said.

"Do all these books have real information in them?" Cathal asked. He looked around, helpless on where he should start.

The worker giggled some more, slightly agitated, but tried to maintain an appropriate composure. "Yes, all nonfiction books have real information. Fiction books are made-up stories." The man nodded to Cathal as he walked away and said, "Enjoy," and then he muttered under his breath, "I'm going to get them back for this."

"Thank you!" said Cathal. He stared at the endless rows of books. He couldn't even fathom how many were before him. "Let's see if this works," he said to himself.

He stepped up to one of the shelves and took out a book titled, *The Rise of Rome*. He opened it up and flipped through the pages. He glanced over hundreds of pages, each with hundreds of words. "How am I ever going to read all this?" he thought and then remembered Crowley had explained something about how he could focus on the book or touch it and all the information from it would magically be engrained into his memory.

It finally dawned on him as to where he was and when. Just hours ago, he was hunting a stag over a thousand years in the past. Crowley said he could travel through time, and if that worked, he might as well try to see if this educational magic would work as well.

He closed the book and his eyes. Holding the book in his hands, he cleared his mind of everything but that book. It started to glow. A bright light shot from the book to his head. He felt the same surge flow through him as he did back in Crowley's hut when he gave him those special abilities. Thousands of bits of information flooded his mind, and then it was over. Out of breath, he opened his eyes. He was shocked that all of a sudden he knew and remembered everything about the rise of the Roman Empire just from focusing on that book.

He was beside himself. To test this phenomenon, he remembered what page started the topic of Rome's brilliant water system. He flipped the book open to that page, and there it was, a description of their aqueducts they created. Cathal placed the book back on the shelf in its proper place. He didn't want to change history in any way, right down to his placement of a book in the library.

He raced through hundreds of books with pure excitement. Moving from section to section, he got so good at this that he stopped picking out individual books; instead, he placed his hands over several spines at a time and acquired the knowledge of multiple books simultaneously.

He learned about all histories, war, combat, science, and even survival in the wild. He was excited to read about the history of Ireland and to see that Brian Boru, a little boy he had met in the woods when he was younger, eventually had become High King of Ireland. Unfortunately, many people had to lose their lives for this to happen, and many villages he knew of were burned to the ground as a result.

As Cathal went book by book, a man in a hooded gray sweatshirt and blue jeans watched intently at him doing all this reading in such a peculiar way. Several people walking by Cathal gave him strange looks and made comments. "Too much drugs," said one.

"It's not Halloween," said another.

Some others made remarks that he hadn't had enough sleep or that he spent too much time studying.

Cathal had so much fun doing this; he even made his way over to some fictional books. "I knew Frodo could do it!" he said, a moment after he had placed *The Return of the King* back on the shelf. Through Cathal's peripheral vision, he thought he saw someone's face watching him through the shelves. He turned his head, glancing in the direction, but saw nothing. An eerie feeling flooded his entire body. "There was definitely someone there," he thought. He moved to that aisle to see if he could catch the face that was watching him, but there was nothing. "Could the evil forces already be following me here?" he thought but quickly shut that idea down since he hadn't done anything yet to cause alarm.

After several hours, Cathal decided to sit at a table and review all that he had learned. He still couldn't get over all the technology the world had today and all the discoveries that had been made. From the discovery of the New World to the invention of flying airplanes, space travel, bombs, and Kung Fu, he realized that much had transpired since his native time period.

He took out his scroll from the satchel and looked at the various dates. He was able to determine exactly where to go for all these dates, based on the knowledge he now possessed. He now understood why Crowley had talked about Chicago and the Prohibition period. "Hmm, first stop—May 23, 1924, Chicago," he said to himself.

CHAPTER SEVEN

Rays of light from the sun crept through thick trees. Leaves shuffled about on the ground below the trees of the forest as a young man wandered aimlessly through the woods. He had a lanky physique. He was tall and pale, with hair slightly mixed with colors of red and brown.

He had made his way about another hundred yards when he paused and noticed the wind had begun to pick up speed drastically. Trees swayed in no general direction; they shifted all over the place, violently jerking from one side to another. *Crack!* He heard a loud sound in the east and dashed toward the noise like any curious young person would.

Quietly, he crept up to where he thought the noise had occurred. Crouching and examining the area from behind a tree safely, the boy saw a man with his back turned, hunched over and moving objects around in a small cave-like hole underneath the roots of a massive tree. The man was wearing a ridiculous outfit, according to the boy, one he had never seen—the attire of a mobster from the 1920s.

The mysterious man stopped what he was doing and stood up looking in one direction. The young boy could now see his side profile and recognized him immediately. It was his cousin.

"Cathal?" he curiously shouted out.

The man in pinstripes jumped around. Shock sprang across his face. "Liam! What are you doing here?"

Cathal tried to act as if the situation was completely normal.

"Cathal, I just walked past this spot not moments ago, and you weren't here." Liam paused to try to collect his thoughts. "And then I heard a loud noise. I ran back, and here you are, clothed in I don't know what, but it's clothing I've never seen. You look very odd."

Cathal winced in pain, favoring his left arm. He could see Liam staring at the wound on his left shoulder. It was a bloody mess.

"Cathal, what is going on?" Liam asked with great confusion. "You're hiding strange objects and wearing odd clothes, and you've been hurt badly. And you appeared out of thin air."

"Relax, it's not what you think," Cathal responded.

"I don't know what to think," Liam continued. "I was literally just here, and you weren't anywhere around. What you are wearing looks hideous. What is going on?"

"I don't know if I can tell you, Liam. I need to get to Crowley as soon as possible. This was a terrible thing. You seeing me like this. But I need your help. Will you help me?" Cathal pressed down on his wound, attempting to keep pressure on it to stop the bleeding.

Liam agreed and helped Cathal as they walked through the forest back to the village. Liam continued to probe him for answers, but Cathal continued to keep quiet about such matters and kept trying to change the subject. Just before they reached the outskirts of the forest, Cathal stopped and said, "You need to get me different clothes. I can't be seen in this."

"What, you don't want anyone to think you've gone completely mad?" Liam smiled.

He agreed and ran into the village. Several minutes later, he came back carrying fresh robes. "These are mine, but they will have to do."

Cathal changed into some of Liam's brown robes. He instantly felt more like his normal self. The material of the suit he had taken off was soft but way too tight and constricting for his taste. "I need to get to Crowley as soon as possible," said Cathal. "Please help me get there."

Together, they walked to his hut. It took everything Cathal had to hold back his pain in his shoulder and walk as if nothing had happened. Just before he was able to knock on the door, Liam stopped and pulled him aside and said, "I want to be involved with whatever you are doing. I can help you. I am going mad here, doing the same thing every day. What you are doing seems dangerous, and you can't do it alone. I'll do whatever it takes."

"I'll see what I can do," said Cathal. "This may be a while. Crowley's not going to like what he hears. Go find something to do." Liam disappeared into the village as Cathal knocked on the door. The door cracked open; Cathal could see that Crowley had noticed Liam in the distance, walking away, as he pulled Cathal inside.

"What happened to your shoulder?" Crowley asked, grabbing Cathal's shoulder. He placed his hand over the wound. The pain began to disappear slowly.

"Wow, you are amazing," said Cathal. Crowley let go as Cathal checked out his shoulder. There was no more pain, and the wound was completely gone. All that remained of the gun wound was the stained blood on his robe.

"What happened? How far are you along?" Crowley questioned. Cathal told Crowley about the library and Chicago and about all the amazing things he had learned about from the future. He also told him how different the future looked where he had been. Crowley smiled a bit. His confidence grew in Cathal's skills and abilities to triumph in this journey.

Crowley also looked annoyed. "I told you not to change history as much as possible...Having a warehouse blown up is a change to history."

Cathal's head lowered in shame. "There was nothing I could do about that. I tried my best."

Crowley placed his hand on Cathal's shoulder in comfort. "I know you did. I'm sorry, this is a great burden. You survived and retrieved the stone."

"The Don in Chicago had some incredible power, like you," said Cathal. "He hurled bolts of blue flames at me. What can you tell me about this? I didn't read about any of this in the books."

"He must have been one of the Tarnen. The Tarnok and the Elluna, the Tarnen and Elluna's Guard, each have a special power. These types of things are withheld from the history books. Elluna's Guard never try to use any of their powers in public, and if the Tarnen use a power, usually any person who witnesses it outside of his or her own ends up dead. Luck must be on your side."

Cathal was very intrigued by these special powers, but he couldn't hide his current predicament any longer: Liam. "Crowley...there's a problem."

Crowley's face was engulfed in stress.

"After I came back from Chicago, I had to hide the stone. Well, Liam spotted me doing this in the forest. And, well, he saw a lot. He saw me wearing clothing from the 1920s and hiding the stone." Crowley's eyes widened and started to turn a shade of red. "Now he's seen things he shouldn't have and is eager to help."

"You imbecile!" said Crowley. "I told you not to let anyone find out about this, and the first moment you get back, precisely that happens!" The words spewed out of Crowley's mouth at such an alarming rate that Cathal had to repeat slowly what he thought he had heard in his head before he could formulate any such reply.

"There was nothing I could do about that. He happened to be in the same spot in the forest where I came back to," Cathal said as he attempted to plead his poor case. "The odds of that happening are immeasurable."

"I told you to find somewhere where no one would wander off to. Apparently, you misjudged." Crowley paced back and forth, kicking his feet across the ground.

"Look, there's nothing I can do about it now. I can't kill him. He's my cousin. I could use some help. Chicago was very dangerous, and I almost didn't make it out alive. I'm not sure if I could do everything on my own. If I train him, he could be useful."

Crowley grunted in disgust. "I beg to differ. He could get you both killed. And he doesn't have the capabilities that you have. He's going to slow you down and surely ruin the whole quest."

"Crowley, please, you know how he is. He will never stop until he gets involved. He will tell the whole village if I don't bring him along."

He sighed. "You are right. But I believe this is a grave mistake. But it is you, not I, who must face these evils. If you feel he will be a benefit to you, then his life is in your hands. You must be careful."

"Thank you, Crowley." He hugged him and walked to the door.

"Bring him to me before you depart," Crowley stated as Cathal left the hut.

Outside, Liam waited impatiently, leaning on the outside wall of a hut across the path. He spotted Cathal and ran directly to him.

"Cathal! What news?" Liam asked as he caught up to him.

"I will call on you later. Be prepared to leave as soon as I say."

They went their own ways. Liam went to finish up chores he had to do around the village, and Cathal made his way to his home.

"Where have you been? You've been missing all night! I was worried sick!" Nora smacked him across his face.

Shocked, Cathal replied, "I'm sorry, Ma. I was out hunting all night."

"And you brought back nothing?"

"It didn't go well. There was nothing to hunt." He downed a large cup of water.

"I'm just glad you're alive. There are rumors of raiders in these lands. You can never be too careful." She'd been saying that to him his whole life whenever he'd be out much later than he was supposed to be.

He needed to cover up the fact that he'd be away for a while with Liam. "I'm taking Liam on a trip. We may be gone for a couple of days. He wants me to teach him how to hunt."

Surprised, she stopped chopping her vegetables. "I'm so happy to hear that. You never really gave Liam much thought over the years. Well, better late than never. Please be careful, dear."

Liam was seventeen years of age, several years younger than Cathal. He was just as curious as Cathal but didn't have the same courage as Cathal to embark on adventures with him. Because of this, Cathal never really gave him much time to bond with him. Hearing this surely shocked his mother, and she was delighted they would finally be spending some time with each other.

"Thanks, Mom. I love you." Cathal ran over to her, hugged her, and quickly snatched some food off the table she was preparing. "I will be back in a couple of days."

He had no idea if what he just said was actually true. Would he be back in a couple of days? Would he ever come back? He didn't like to think of such things, but these questions would still creep back into his thoughts from time to time. He just knew he had to stay focused to rescue the world.

"Be safe! I love you too!" Nora waved as he left.

Cathal stepped out into the cool fresh air. Keela waved to him from across the village with three of her fingers. He smiled and gave the same back to her. As he started to make his way toward her, she motioned him to stop and to meet her at her place. He followed her from behind, trailing a few yards back to keep their affection for each other a secret from the rest of the village, but mainly her father. She entered her hut, and soon after, he did also.

She ran and jumped into his arms, and fingers intertwined, they kissed passionately as if they hadn't seen each other in years. Cathal stopped and leaned back. He gently ran his fingertips down her face as she smiled, staring deeply into his eyes.

"You can't stay long," she said finally. "My father will be back soon."

Cathal sighed. "Even if we were married, your father will hate the thought."

"He has to say yes. He has no choice," she replied immediately, yet uncertainty lingered in her voice.

"What he doesn't know won't hurt him." He smiled and got down on one knee, gently holding her hands. "I love you, always have, and always will. Marry me. Grow old with me. Raise some young ones with me. I'll do everything I can to keep you safe forever. You are my everything, my heaven."

Keela went down to his level, smiled more than ever, and began to kiss him. "Yes, of course, forever, and ever I will be yours!"

They were interrupted by the sounds of her father grunting outside; he was getting closer and closer.

Startled, he kissed her one last time and then said, "See you later!" He ran to the open window and dove out. His head reappeared through the window. "I have to go away for a couple of days. I will come back for you. I promise. I love you."

They kissed again, and he went off.

The door opened, and she spun around, smiling. "Why are you so happy, Keela?" her father asked. "Does cooking make you happy?"

Still smiling, she nodded and started to prepare their meal.

With butterflies still shooting back and forth in his stomach, Cathal headed toward Liam's hut. So much was still running through his head. Should he just give up and run away with Keela? He hoped his promise to her was true and that he would come back for her. It was killing him deep inside knowing that he couldn't tell her anything.

"Cathal!" Liam rushed to him from behind.

"Let's go see Crowley. He has a lot to tell you."

Crowley continued to pace back and forth in his hut. It was as if he hadn't stopped since Cathal had left. Soon Cathal and Liam arrived, and Crowley began to speak. "Liam, I wish you never saw Cathal in the forest. You have no idea what you've gotten yourself into. This is not a game, and it is far more dangerous than anything you could possibly imagine. Just the mere fact that you are going to know about these things could possibly get you killed or change the course of history forever. You must never tell anyone what you are about to hear."

Liam eagerly nodded.

"Wipe that grin off your face," said Crowley.

Crowley went on to explain to him everything about the Great War, the scroll, and the bracelet.

Liam was struck with silence. This information was way more than he ever could have imagined. What he had envisioned Cathal doing and what was actually happening were complete opposites. "I think we should get going," Cathal said as he patted Liam on the shoulder. Liam snapped out of his daze and agreed.

"If you are ready to do so, then make your way. Make sure you cover your tracks and destroy anything other than the stone that you brought back from Chicago."

They gave their good-byes and went on their way.

"Liam, run home quickly, and pack some spare robes so that when we need to come back, we don't have to sneak back into the village every time," Cathal told Liam as they both nodded and ran off, and after gathering their things, they met up when they were ready.

Cathal and Liam made their way deep into the woods up the mountainside. All they could see was the light of their torch on the ground. Darkness surrounded them. "Crowley told me that you could travel with me as long as you were holding on to me as I traveled through time," said Cathal.

"I still won't believe this is all true until it actually happens. Where are we going again?"

"Nanking, China. Terrible things happened there in the twentieth century. We need to be ready for anything and everything."

Liam's mouth dropped. "The twentieth century? That's about one thousand years into the future!"

"Shh, we don't know who is out here. We need to keep it down, and yes, the bracelet actually works. I've already been to the twentieth century once."

Conversing together, they walked a few more minutes through the dark woods until Cathal stopped abruptly and said, "Here we are. Put your spare clothes over here." They both placed their clothes underneath some bushes. Cathal walked over to the small cave underneath the large tree. "Here it is. This is where we will be hiding the stones." He lifted up some branches to reveal the stone.

Liam's eyes widened as he said, "This is where I found you earlier." The flame from the torch reflected off the stone, and a mixture of flames and darkness spread over the stone. Liam reached down and rubbed his hand over it. It was perfect in shape, and Cathal knew exactly what Liam was feeling at this point. The stone felt as though you were running your fingers across perfectly smooth glass.

"This is incredible," Liam said. "There are four more?"

"Yes, I almost died for the first one, and for some reason, I don't believe it is going to get any easier. If you're going to come along, you need to listen to me and do everything I say for our own safety."

Liam agreed.

Cathal lit a fire for the night. He threw his mobster outfit from before into the fire. They watched as it disappeared into the flames. They continued to converse, and Cathal described to Liam his visit to the library and his encounter in Chicago. He also filled him in on the necessary information he would need about the Nanking situation.

"I can't believe such things happened," Liam responded to Cathal's description of the event.

"You're right. It was called The Rape of Nanking for a reason. Unfortunately, there were many other terrible events throughout history, and this was just one of them," Cathal replied.

Eventually, the fire blew out, and they went to sleep, resting up for the dangers awaiting them.

CHAPTER EIGHT

New York City, USA—January 20, 1999

Heavy steps echoed down a dark hallway, lit only by the light coming from an office at its end. The fire still burned deep within Skorn's eyes from that Chicago blast. His eyes were worn through years of experiencing and administering pain.

Skorn's life had never been an easy one. Born in 1972, his biological parents had left him at an orphanage when he was just a baby and had never looked back. He was placed in different foster homes throughout his childhood. For one reason or another, none of the foster kids had liked him and had often manipulated the foster parents into hating him as well. Most of his foster parents were drunken alcoholics, and he'd receive nightly beatings from them for some lie told by another child or for merely breathing too loud. He had only been able to take so much of this, and by the time he was twelve, Skorn had run away.

He had spent three years surviving on the streets of New York City as a homeless person, living hand to mouth. That was until one fateful day in 1987, when a man named Troy had saved him and had taken him in. He had been in a back alley, taking a beating that brought him to the brink of death, when Troy had intervened. Skorn had been amazed by the way Troy had handled the man with ease, as the man had run off cowering. Troy had offered Skorn shelter, and he had accepted. It had been the first genuine act of kindness Skorn had received in his first fifteen years of life.

For several years, Troy had supported Skorn with a home, the nurturing he never had, and had taught him how to defend himself. When Skorn was of the proper age, Troy had made him enlist into the US Army. He had rapidly advanced through the ranks. He had then been recruited into Delta Force at an early age and had become a member of a Black Ops program shortly after. They had used him on many missions as a highly skilled assassin. Skorn had the ability, far greater than anyone else, to sneak in, terminate the mark, and escape without the enemy having any knowledge.

Ultimately, the time had come when Troy had convinced Skorn that he had work to be done of far greater importance, and he had left the military. Troy had taught him the true teachings of the Tarnen, and he had learned of the Great War and the God Stones. Once he had been fully initiated into the Tarnen, the Tarnen had discovered Skorn's special power that allowed him to travel through time. Troy felt he was the perfect candidate to stop Cathal. He had the same ability that Cathal had, and he had become a trained killer. Skorn had been stalking Cathal ever since.

"Close the door behind you," a voice behind a large black leather chair said as puffs of smoke ascended into the air from the voice, facing the city skyline.

The office was designed mainly of dark-stained wood; bookshelves lined the right and left walls. In front of Skorn was a large wooden desk, probably from the eighteen hundreds. Beyond the desk was a large, black leather chair, facing a wall, which was all one gigantic window. From this chair, one could see every major triumph of architecture New York City had to offer.

"What did you find, Skorn?" the mysterious voice asked, still facing the windows at the night sky.

"He's very clumsy. I can take him out now. I've observed him twice. I saw him once at a library at the University of Delaware, and then I followed him to Chicago in the 1920s. He did acquire the Earth Stone, but he nearly got himself killed."

Skorn lowered his head in shame.

The chair spun around. A large man with slicked-back gray hair, glasses, and an expensive suit was in the chair, smoking a large cigar. "Don't underestimate him, Skorn. It was his first trial, and he passed it. He even survived the Don. How is this so?"

Staring at the large cigar, Skorn nervously answered, "It was weird. In the library, he was doing something very odd. He kept touching different books on the cover, and then he would get excited about them. He wouldn't even open them up to read them."

Skorn walked up to the bookshelf on the left wall. He stared intently at the spines of the books. He touched them in the same manner Cathal did in the library, wondering what was going on during that time. "I watched him infiltrate the warehouse. It was as if he had years of training experience in real-life scenarios. He was highly skilled in combat and weapons. How is this possible, coming from a mere boy from tenth-century Ireland?"

"You say that after every book he touched, he seemed to get excited." Troy placed his cigar on the tray near his computer. "I've heard of the ability to touch books and learn everything from them in a matter of seconds. I've never actually known someone who could do such a thing. This must be his power. He had an ability to absorb anything with extreme haste because the bracelet is what helps him move through time."

Troy stood up, walked toward the windowed wall, and placed a hand on the glassy surface. "Skorn, I didn't get to where I am by running into things blind. Meticulous planning, persistence, and ruthlessness are what got me here. I want you to continue to study him and his methods. Follow him and watch him from afar in Nanking. Just observe him. This should be a greater test for Cathal. I doubt he can get by a bloodthirsty army like that."

"Can't I just kill him?" Skorn asked. Impatience flowed through his words.

"No! We aren't sure of his extent in skills. It was only his first trial. This absorption ability has me vexed. You may need to bring some help from The Six."

Skorn interrupted with a laugh, "He's so sloppy with his skills. I don't need their help at all."

"That's enough! You will go to China and only observe, again. If he is successful there, I want you to follow him back to his village. I want you to find out everything about him. What does he do? Where does he live? And who are his loved ones? There must be someone from Elluna's Guard watching over him, guiding him. Identify who that is. Find out everything you can, and report back to me immediately."

Troy picked up the cigar and gave another large puff.

"I will do as you say." Skorn bowed his head to Troy and headed for the hallway.

"Be patient, Skorn," Troy said as he took one more puff and smothered the cigar in his hand. Skorn disappeared into the darkness.

CHAPTER NINE

Nanking, China—December 15, 1937

The aisles that once contained food and other household products now lay scattered on the floor. The products had been smashed or thrown about. Flurries blew in through the shattered windows and broken-down walls. The ground shook; the cracks in the walls began to extend as debris rained down from the ceiling. A bright blue light flashed in the center of this ruined abandoned store, throwing the store products in all directions. Cathal and a shaken Liam appeared in place of the light.

"Oh my lord, that was incredible!" Liam screamed as the ground shook from bombs exploding in another part of the city.

Liam and Cathal were surrounded by rubble; small paths made it possible for them to maneuver the aisles without making too much noise. "Shh, we need to be quiet and keep to ourselves at all cost," whispered Cathal. "The enemy is all around us—an entire army."

They heard screams coming through the openings in the walls and windows. The sounds of women and children crying and men yelling rang out in the street. Crouching to stay out of sight, they quickly made their way toward the window to see.

What they saw was the first of many things that no one on earth would ever want to witness, know of, or certainly experience. Japanese soldiers marched staggering men, women, and children in lines toward a designated spot. One man was pulled out of his line and beaten to a bloody pulp as his wife and child screamed in horror. There was a gunshot, and the man lay on the floor motionless. Cathal and Liam both cringed.

The city streets were blanketed in blood, debris, limbs, and, in some areas, piles of dead bodies. The flurries provided a poor attempt to cover up the carnage. Cathal and Liam couldn't see where the soldiers were taking the rest of the civilians.

Liam stood up and ran toward the other room. "That's a bad idea," whispered Cathal as he reached out to stop him, but it was too late. He could see Liam from the other room frozen in one spot, arms beginning to rise. Someone else was in that room, shouting at Liam as he struggled to comprehend what the man was saying.

Cathal could understand. It was a Japanese soldier, and he was about to lose all patience with Liam.

The soldier's patience ran its course with Liam's lack of response; he moved closer to Liam, jamming the handgun into the side of his head. Liam certainly understood this form of communication and went down on both knees, shaking.

Cathal quietly lifted a heavy piece of concrete from the rubble and crept into the room adjacent to them. The soldier continued to shout directions at Liam, who didn't understand. Cathal crept closer from behind as the soldier's demands got louder and louder. Liam cried out, "I don't know what you want!"

Just as the soldier placed a whistle in his mouth to alert the others, Cathal swung and connected the heavy concrete rubble with the back of the soldier's head. The soldier went straight to the floor, immobile.

"What did he have in his hand?" Liam gasped for breath. He obviously felt shock at how quickly he had already jeopardized the covertness of the mission.

"I told you we need to stick together! It's far too dangerous for you to do anything without my command! And it's a gun. It's like a bow but a lot more dangerous."

"I'm terribly sorry. It will never happen again!" Liam apologized as he quickly hugged Cathal. "Thank you, you saved my life!"

They could hear more shouting from the window, and they ran over to get a better look. The men, women, and children who were marching before were now lined up along the city wall. Groups of them were huddled together, holding their loved ones and crying or praying for someone or something to rescue them.

Together, several troops aimed their machine guns at the crowd and opened fire. Cathal and Liam couldn't stomach what they saw, but neither could they look away from the dreadful view before them. Bullets and screams rang out, while the soldiers cackled. Blood splattered all over the walls behind them and the ground. The whole area was painted in blood. Not one person was left alive.

"We must do something, Cathal!" Liam pleaded with him.

"Liam, this is extremely horrifying, but as much as we want to help stop this, it is happening. We can't stop this event from happening. If we try to, it could change the rest of history and possibly eliminate our chances of ever acquiring all the stones. Our only priority, as terrible as it seems, is to take back all the stones."

"I guess you're right," Liam agreed, but his face was filled with frustration. "I'm sorry. I'm still trying to comprehend the magnitude of all this."

"The stones are going to help us stop anything like this from happening again," Cathal said, trying to reassure him. Even though Cathal didn't truly believe what he was saying, he needed to be strong for his cousin. "We need to change our clothes and get out of these robes."

Cathal walked over to the guard and undressed him. He took his own robes off and changed into the soldier's uniform. "I will be a guard, and you will be my prisoner," he stated as he finished tying up the unconscious guard.

"I really think that's a bad idea—me being a prisoner. This could cause some serious issues."

Cathal moved from room to room, searching for more clothes. "We have no other option. Unless we find another soldier, I believe it's going to be a lot easier for us to get civilian clothes. You'll be my prisoner whom I am transporting so we can walk freely through the city at a distance."

They entered a back storage room of the store. A rank stench of death filled their noses. The ground shook, and Liam and Cathal grabbed the walls for balance. "Bombs," Cathal stated.

They scanned the entire room and saw the remains of three people in the corner. As they got closer to the bodies, the type of horror that had happened there became much clearer.

It seemed to be a father, a mother, and their daughter. The father was lying dead prostrate, with several bullet holes on his back. He was on top of a teenage girl. She had a bullet hole in her head. The mother lay with what seemed to be knife wounds through the stomach.

"They must have tortured this family before they ended their lives. Horrible." Cathal analyzed the situation, while Liam ran to the far corner and began to throw up.

Cathal took off the clothes from the father, trying so desperately not to look at anything but the clothes. "Here, put these on. You'll be my prisoner whom I'm transporting."

Liam cleaned himself up and changed on the other side of the room, making sure not to look at the carnage.

"The stone has to be kept somewhere safe. I assume it would be with a General or someone else who is of a high rank in charge of this campaign. We need to look for a place that is heavily guarded," Cathal explained.

Cathal grabbed Liam and pressed the soldier's gun into his back. "Don't worry. It's for show," said Cathal. Liam took a big gulp and nodded. Cathal pressed the barrel against the middle of his back as they walked out the backdoor.

Outside the store, the city had the same look that the store had: it looked as though it had been a prosperous place at one time but was now mainly rubble. Cathal forced his prisoner through the war-torn streets as the sounds of bullets, bombs, and screams echoed through their ears. Heads tilted downward, they moved along as they studied their surroundings, looking for something that could lead them to the stone.

"Stop." Cathal grabbed Liam and threw him against the wall of a partially destroyed building. "I hear some guards laughing."

Cathal moved to the edge of the building and peeked around the corner.

"That was the seventeenth today!" the guard bragged to the other as he wiped the blood from his sword on the headless body's shoulder.

"I need to catch up! This will only be twelve for me!" the other guard said and raised his sword and sliced right through the neck of a crying man, kneeling on the ground. The head slid right down the side of the neck, opposite to where the body fell over, and rolled right next to the other head.

Cathal turned away and looked directly into Liam's eyes. He thought what he saw through the window of the store was the worst he would have to witness, but he started to second-guess that statement. "They are cutting people's heads off..." Cathal struggled to get more words out. "We need to find another route."

Just as he grabbed Liam to pull him in another direction, the ground shook some more. This shaking didn't stop like the bombs from before; it was much different, and much closer. They crouched down.

Two tanks rolled down the road on the only other possible route they could take compared to going past the two soldiers who had just beheaded the civilians. "I guess we are going to have to take our chances with the swords. Keep your mouth shut. Don't say anything. Even if we are spotted, and they ask you questions, let me answer," Cathal ordered.

Liam swallowed a big gulp as Cathal pressed the gun against him, pushing him out into the open. They walked unnoticed past the soldiers, who were still busy admiring their murderous acts. They had almost reached the next building, when Liam accidentally kicked a rock. The soldiers immediately whipped around and stared straight at them.

"Stop right there!" Both guards rushed over to meet Cathal and Liam, whose heads were tilted down and facing away from them. "Where are you taking this one?"

Cathal slowly turned around and began to speak to the two guards. He kept his face partially hidden from the two soldiers to try to keep away the visual that he wasn't Japanese. Cathal spoke fluently in Japanese to the soldiers, while Liam kept his face hidden from the soldiers' view. "I've got my orders to bring him to the river for execution."

"Oh, that's no fun!" said the soldiers. "All right, move along. Sorry to keep you waiting!"

Cathal nodded as he violently pushed Liam away from the soldiers and in the direction they had been going.

"Wait!" A smile grew on one soldier's face as he pulled out his sword. "We've been killing them all day with our swords. It's quite something else to take a life with a sword instead of using a gun. Do you want to try?"

He held out the sword to Cathal.

"I'm under strict orders to get him to the river. Apparently, one of the men there has had a personal issue with this man and wanted to take care of it himself." Cathal tried to work his way out of this decision.

"No, no, no. I insist." He moved closer to Cathal and pressed the sword's handle to his chest until Cathal grabbed it. "We will all say that there was an accident, and you couldn't get him to the river."

The other guard nodded, agreeing to his partner's idea, and walked over to Liam, pushing him to his knees.

Cathal placed his gun carefully on the ground. He gripped the sword tightly with both hands. "I really don't want to disobey orders."

The guards didn't seem to care what he said.

"Do it, or I'll do it for you," remarked one of the soldiers. "I'd love to reach eighteen decapitations for the day."

Liam turned around and looked up at Cathal. He looked so confused about what they all said in Japanese and why Cathal was holding a sword. All he could do was to face the ground. He closed his eyes and began to pray.

Cathal readied his swing for Liam's head. One of the guards kept staring back and forth between both of their partially hidden faces. He whispered something to the other soldier, getting him to study both of their faces quickly.

Cathal raised the sword with both hands, priming to strike down on Liam.

"Stop!" The soldier rapidly pulled out a gun and aimed it at Cathal. "Drop the sword now!"

CHAPTER TEN

"Where are you from?" demanded the soldier, his gun directed straight at Cathal with both his hands raised. "You don't look like you're one of us. Drop the sword!"

Cathal lowered the sword slowly, but right before he was about to place it on the ground, he hurled it straight at one of the soldiers, penetrating one right in the chest.

Before the other soldier had enough time to take his gun out, Cathal dashed for the falling man, ripped the sword out of his chest, and swung at the other guard, striking him down. Bullets flew into the air.

The shouts of other soldiers could be heard from behind a building about a block away. "Quick, we need to hide!" Cathal rushed over to Liam, lifting him to his feet. They quickly jumped behind a small barricade and crouched behind it, hiding from view.

Footsteps drew closer. They heard two men shouting at each other as they started to survey the area. One blew his whistle. "Shh, don't call anyone. They are still here, and we don't want to alarm them," the other guard said.

They continued their search on the grounds. The footsteps grew louder as one walked straight up to the barricade. Cathal's and Liam's hearts skipped a beat; they prayed that the soldier, who was now standing right above them, would move on. He looked out past the barricade and saw nothing odd, so he turned around. Cathal quickly stood up and grabbed the man by his neck, pulling him over the barricade and knocking him out. Cathal pulled the gun out of the man's hands.

Multiple bombs exploded in the distance as Cathal fired at the other soldier already firing back at him. Bullets flew at him, but all of them missed. Cathal finally placed two in his chest, and the soldier fell to the ground. "The bomb sounds hid all the gunfire. No one should be coming back. But we need to hide the bodies," Cathal stated.

They quickly dragged the remaining three bodies over the barricade where they would remain hidden. Liam stared at the bodies and said, "I don't think the prisoner idea is working anymore. Can I change into a soldier as well?"

Cathal agreed, and Liam quickly undressed from his civilian outfit into his new bloody soldier attire.

They continued to make their way through the streets, walking with confidence like the other military men. Still, they kept their heads slightly tilted downward just in case. As they went through the streets, Cathal made a quick mental observation of a building storing large canisters of gasoline.

Making it to the outskirts of the city, they started to walk parallel to the river's current. They saw soldiers stacking bodies—whole and parts of bodies—up against a wall. Men were buried up to their necks, getting kicked, urinated on, lit on fire, shot, or buried alive. Liam grabbed Cathal's arm and squeezed in anger, but he didn't say anything to cause attention, and they continued walking.

The horrible music in the air continued to be filled with a mixture of explosions, gunshots, and screams. What they saw next made them stop dead in their tracks.

A family of three boys, a girl, and their parents were lined up along the Yangtze River's side. Heads down, they were holding hands and crying. The soldiers opened heavy fire on them; their bodies flew back into the red river, joining other bodies that had already been flowing downstream.

This moment was bittersweet for them. It was terribly hard watching a helpless family get executed, but as their bodies fell into the river, the view that opened up behind them allowed them to see exactly what they had been looking for.

"That's it. That's where the stone will be," Cathal quietly whispered to Liam. "Across the river, that cave."

A cave entrance could be seen from across the river with six armed men. One of them looked to be a general, giving orders to five others. Cathal quickly formulated a plan and explained. "We need a distraction to get them away from that entrance. I'm going to run off and see what I can do. You need to stay here and hide."

Liam gave Cathal a hesitant look. "Liam, trust me. Hide right behind this bridge, but keep an eye on the soldiers guarding the cave entrance. When I come back, I'm going to need to know where they are."

Before Liam could say another word, Cathal was running off back into the war-torn city. Liam quickly ran over to the side of a half pillar, which supported the bridge, and crouched down behind it to stay hidden.

Cathal quickly ran through the broken streets to the corner of a building. From there, he could see right inside the building where he had spotted the gasoline canisters earlier. Inside, several men were standing at a table, pointing down toward it, deep in discussion. "Must be a map. I need to get in there," Cathal said to himself and scanned down the street just a bit more, where he saw a jeep parked several buildings away.

He dashed across the street toward the jeep. As he got closer, he was able to make out a man sleeping in the backseat. Cathal silently approached the truck and sat in the driver's seat. The key was in the ignition. He turned on the jeep, and even with the noise and the shaking of the engine, the soldier remained asleep.

Cathal drove the jeep directly toward the building with the canisters, his foot pressed down on the accelerator. The jeep's speed increased every moment.

All of a sudden, he lost control. His neck felt as though it was being crushed in a vice. He was losing oxygen fast. The soldier had awoken and now had his hands wrapped around his neck, trying to choke him.

Cathal tried to fight back with one hand and continue to drive the jeep with the other. Continuously punching the man from behind to fight free, he lost complete control of the vehicle. The jeep swerved and flipped sideways as it smashed through the brick wall of the building, sending the soldier flying over the canisters.

The flying debris and crashing jeep knocked down all the other men in the room. Cathal's right leg was now pinned. He fought to break free. What he saw next motivated him much more to get out of his current position. The canisters were now leaking and spilling gasoline all over the ground. A fire started in the hood of the jeep. Cathal pulled harder and harder, freeing his leg enough to climb out. He pulled himself out from beneath the jeep. The fire was spreading further down the hood, spreading toward the gasoline-covered floor.

Faster than he had ever moved before, he popped up to his feet and hobbled out into the street, and at the last possible moment, he dove toward the ground as an explosion sent fire and rubble out in all directions. This was followed by an enormous explosion, collapsing the entire building and sending more rubble and smoke in every direction. Cathal was engulfed in the flames and smoke.

CHAPTER ELEVEN

The second explosion knocked Liam to his back. He looked to the sky, and all he saw were towering flames and black smoke. "That was the direction Cathal ran," he thought. This put him in full panic mode, if he hadn't already been so.

He heard shouting behind him, and he turned back and saw the general giving out orders, which he didn't understand. The general pointed at two guards, and they solidified their positions by guarding the entrance. The other two soldiers took off with the general over the bridge in the direction of the blast.

Liam sat and waited for Cathal. Minutes went by; they seemed like hours to him. He continued to monitor the two soldiers, who appeared stone cold. They hadn't moved an inch. In the other direction, he continued to see more and more soldiers run straight for the burning building.

"Come on, Cathal. Where are you?" Liam thought. "You need to make it out of there alive."

After about ten minutes—which felt like a day to Liam—he had given up on Cathal and decided to move on. Liam stood up and turned to make his way toward the cave entrance. But he couldn't move; his foot was locked in place. He looked down to see a hand clasped over his foot; his eyes followed up the arm to see a face covered in ash. It was Cathal.

"It worked! We need to get inside that cave before they get back," Cathal said.

Liam looked extremely excited and thankful to see Cathal again as he pulled Cathal to his feet.

"We can't just cross the bridge. We have to go under," ordered Cathal as Liam followed him underneath the bridge.

They made their way across the river, swimming underneath the bridge to stay hidden from the guards. Along the way, they bumped into several human corpses that passed them in the current. Reaching the other side of the river, they crawled up the hill and crept past the guards and off to the side of the woods, adjacent to the cave.

"What's the plan from here?" Liam asked as they crouched behind some thick tree trunks, observing the two guards standing still as statues at the cave entrance.

"Do you see that hill behind the cave that leads up to the top of its entrance?" Cathal asked Liam, who nodded. Cathal continued to explain the plan. "We are going to get up there and jump down on top of the guards for a surprise attack. You take one, and I take the other. We should be able to take them out without causing alarm this way."

They quietly moved their way through the woods until they were directly behind the cave. Cathal got into a prone position and began to crawl up the hill. Liam imitated his cousin's every move.

Reaching the top edge of the cave, they saw both men in the same spot they were before. Cathal motioned to Liam, and they both jumped down. Cathal hit his guard perfectly, knocking him out on impact. Liam wasn't as successful and failed, as his attack merely pushed the man off balance and out of the way. The soldier recovered quickly and began to beat down on Liam, who tried to defend himself. Cathal ran up from behind and put the guard into a chokehold, bringing him to the ground. As the guard attempted to fight off Cathal's hold, the guard's body eventually went limp.

"I'm so sorry again!" Liam said as he received an annoyed look from Cathal.

Cathal grabbed his guard's body and dragged him into the cave and said, "Quick, we have to get them out of sight!"

Liam pulled his guard in and out of sight right after Cathal.

They made sure they placed both bodies where no one could see them and then started to walk cautiously deeper into the cave. The cave went a few yards before they reached an area that appeared to be the commander's quarters.

A lantern sat on a table, dimly lighting up the area. To their right, a cot was pressed up against a rock wall. The center of the room had a table with a lantern and a map filled with markers strategically positioned. Beyond the table, there was a desk pushed up against another rocky wall. There was no chest visible anywhere, and there was nothing there that gave away the possible location of one of the stones.

Both searched around the dark room. They found a couple of ammunition canisters stacked along the wall. They opened each and every canister, but they were all filled with ammo. The stone wasn't there.

"It has to be here. We can't give up just yet. Let's split the room and look more carefully," Cathal said and walked along the rocky walls, feeling around for some secret compartment, while Liam moved back toward the bed and desk, rummaging through each drawer.

Another explosion outside somewhere in town caused pieces of dirt and rock to rain down on their heads. "I'm not sure how much longer we have in here before we are caved in. We really need to hur—" Cathal was interrupted by Liam shouting in excitement.

"I found it! Over here!" Liam said as he crawled out from underneath the bed, holding another open ammunition canister. "It's beautiful!"

Cathal reached into the canister and pulled out a God Stone. Their eyes transfixed on the obsidian nature of the stone, which was just as dark and mirrorlike as the Earth Stone recovered in Chicago. The shape was an exact replica of the previous one and shaped like a quarter of a doughnut. The only difference between the two was the symbol carved on both sides. This one had three wavy, staggered markings, while the one in Chicago had four staggered arrowheads. "This must be water," Liam stated as Cathal smiled and placed the stone in his sack and threw it over his shoulder.

Another explosion sent a lot more dirt and rocks to the floor. "We've got to get out of here now!" Cathal shouted. They ran all the way to the entrance and were immediately stopped by something extremely unexpected.

Meeting them at the entrance was a man unlike any they had seen here in China. The man was clothed in blue jeans and a hooded gray sweatshirt covering most of his face. Snow fell rapidly and heavily behind him. His head tilted up, and staring straight at Cathal and smiling, he said, "You just won't die. Will you? Not in Chicago, and not here."

Cathal, completely puzzled, began to shake nervously. "What? How do you know about Chicago? Who are you?"

The man continued to smile. He pulled the hood back over his head, revealing his face. He was clean-shaven and had short brown hair. His eyes looked worn, years beyond his young facial features. "My name is Skorn, and the only reason I am telling you this is because your time ends here. And I want you to know the name of the person who will see to your failure and death. Now hand over the stone."

Liam dashed straight for him and swung at his head. Still smiling, Skorn ducked with ease and countered with a kick to the head. Liam fell to the ground as limp as the stacks of bodies on the other side of the river. The hooded man placed all his attention on Cathal once more. "Well?" Skorn said, and he reached out his hand, waiting for the stone.

Cathal dropped the sack and charged him. They exchanged several equal blows to the upper body. Skorn laughed as he blocked many of Cathal's attacks. Skorn grabbed both of Cathal's fists, head-butted him, and threw him over his shoulder, slamming him to the ground.

Meanwhile, Liam had just begun to regain consciousness and feeling. Cathal struggled, gasping for the air that was knocked out of him. Skorn made his way for the bag and picked it up. "I'll be taking this," he said.

An assault of gunfire on their location followed shouts from across the river. One connected with Skorn in the arm, causing him to drop the sack and run for cover. More shouting and gunfire continued to fly past their bodies.

"We're being fired on! We have to get the stone and go deep into the woods!" Cathal said as he crawled on the ground toward Liam.

"I'm good. Let's do this!" Liam felt a rush of adrenaline.

They both quickly hopped to their feet and sprinted for the bag as Cathal threw it over his shoulder and ran into the woods, still dodging bullets.

There weren't any paths in the forest that they ran to next, so they had to deal with many obstacles along the way, and they had to run over many roots sticking out of the ground and boulders, which they either jumped over or ran around.

The gunfire never stopped, and the shouting never got lower. They were being stalked by a small group of soldiers through the woods. Bullets kept soaring by, just missing their heads and hitting trees they had just went by or were approaching; the soldiers continued to pursue them.

As they ran, an explosion from the right sent Cathal and Liam flying to the left. As they looked up, a loud cracking sound from above warned them of an enormous tree crashing down toward them. They both rolled out of the way on opposite sides of the tree. Liam got up on the farther side and continued to run away. Cathal rose on the side closest to the firing. He could see the soldiers' faces now; they were much closer than before. The shots came closer and closer as he ran, following Liam from behind.

They came to the end of the woods. An open field of high grass was before them. "In! We must hide here!" Cathal commanded as he ran past Liam.

Liam followed him into the field, where grass smacked them in the face, and bugs flew at them from every direction. They had run about fifty yards, when Cathal ordered Liam to stop and get down. "Listen…" Cathal whispered.

The firing had stopped. They heard nothing but the nature around them. "What are we looking for?" Liam asked.

"Shh, wait."

They heard the quiet sound of grass bending and breaking. The footsteps and sounds began to get louder and louder. The men were getting closer and closer. Cathal and Liam lay down in the muddy ground to camouflage themselves.

Just as they saw their pursuers' boots, the ground began to shake. A loud shrieking sound came from the sky above. The soldiers looked up and started firing upward into the air. Cathal and Liam looked up and saw a comet fly straight overhead, firing lightning bolts down toward the soldiers. And in one moment, the firing had stopped. The bodies of the soldiers fell to the ground, completely charred from the bolts.

They couldn't believe what they had just seen. Did that comet really just take out each soldier individually? Both stood up and saw the burnt bodies of their pursuers on the ground, dead through the thick grass.

"What about the other guy, Skorn?" Liam asked.

"I don't know, but I don't want to wait around to find out. We need to see what that thing is."

Cathal didn't pause to rethink his decision, and his eyes followed the direction of the comet. Liam grabbed his shoulder and shouted, "Are you crazy? You said, 'Get the stone and leave.' We have the stone. There's no other reason for us to be here!"

"Whatever that was, it just saved our lives. We need to find out what it was!" Cathal said as he pulled at Liam. "Let's go!"

They both headed further into the brush, chasing after the comet.

CHAPTER TWELVE

Exhausted from all the events that had taken place, they continued to push through the tall grasses toward the area they thought the comet had gone. In time, the field ended, and the forest began again.

Not long after they entered the woods, they stumbled upon an area with small fragments of burning fire all around. Small flames leapt on the sides of tree trunks, on their leaves, and on the ground below. Surrounded by the fallen trees was a perfectly large bowl-shaped hole in the ground, but there was nothing there to see.

"I need to speak to Viktor." It was an overwhelmingly magnificent voice, echoing from behind.

They both immediately spun around, startled. A large unnatural bright glow stood before them. Cathal and Liam had to shield their eyes as if they were staring directly into the sun. "Why do you think I would know such a person?" Cathal asked this being.

The light began to dim, and in its place stood a large man, extremely muscular in physique. He was draped in white cloth; silvery hair flowed naturally from his head as if there was a constant breeze on him. A large, glowing bow hung across his back. "I am Gabriel, Captain of the Outer Rim Guard, protector and watcher of the skies. You have one of the stones in your possession, and I don't sense Terranos's influence clouding your mind. You must be part of Elluna's Guard."

They both stood awestruck.

"What are your names? We haven't much time to waste. You need to help me this instant. Where is Viktor?" Gabriel's rapid questions left Liam stumped. The boy was still entranced from the man's flowing hair.

Cathal began to reflect about prior conversations with Crowley. He did remember Crowley briefly informing him about the Outer Rim Guard. "My name is Cathal, and this is my cousin, Liam. I have a question— if you're from the Outer Rim Guard, then doesn't that mean that the Tarnok are on their way back?"

Gabriel's impatience with them started to take over. "That is correct, like I said. We have no time. They are indeed coming. Where is Viktor?"

"I'm sorry to say this, but Viktor hasn't been around for many years, and his whereabouts, I am told, are unknown," Cathal answered reluctantly.

Gabriel's head lowered. "I see."

Cathal continued, "I am from another time and land. I've been assigned the task of taking back the stones from the Tarnen. I'm from Ireland, in the year 947. There is a wise man there, named Crowley, who has been guiding me all the way. I believe he is a member of Elluna's Guard. I will speak to him about you and what has occurred. He should know what to do."

"Where is the next stone?" Gabriel's frustration dissipated.

"We're following the Mongolian army. I plan to take back the stone at the Battle of Legnica, in the Kingdom of Poland, on April 9, 1241."

"A battle?" Gabriel couldn't hide the concerned look on his face. "That could be very dangerous. I'll go a day earlier to scout out the situation. Until we meet again, Cathal, Liam…"

Gabriel looked at both and started to glow again.

Cathal and Liam covered their eyes. A loud crack resounded in the air, and the glow of the light shot into the air again through the trees and disappeared.

"Do we trust this fellow?" Liam tried to calm down from what had just happened.

"Yes, the Outer Rim Guard are on our side. And it looks like we could use all the help we can get. Look at what he did to those soldiers. Crowley and I shall fill you in back home."

"Aye, but he can do the same to us!"

"He won't. He was created by Viktor to serve Viktor and the Elluna. He will aid us in finding the stones." Cathal grabbed ahold of Liam's arm. They began to glow of bright blue and disappeared.

About fifty yards away, his back resting against a tree and remaining as quiet as ever, Skorn smiled that same devious smile. "Time to make a visit," he said.

The smile vanished in thin air as several Japanese soldiers reached the area they had all just been looking for to find nothing but a large hole in the ground.

CHAPTER THIRTEEN

Ireland—May 17, AD 947

The sun's early morning rays radiated through the cracks of the trees, covering the forest and coloring the ground in a mixture of red and orange. The trees swirled about as a loud crack echoed in the previously quiet atmosphere. Liam and Cathal appeared out of nowhere.

"Over here," said Cathal. He ran over to the spot under the roots where he had hid the other God Stone and moved some branches and leaves around. He dropped the satchel and carefully pulled out the Water Stone and placed it next to the Earth Stone.

"How many more again?" asked Liam.

Cathal covered up the stones. "We have to get fire, wind, and Viktor's stone to complete our mission."

"Let's get going back to the village." Liam started to walk away toward the village.

"Are you serious? Look at ourselves." Cathal pointed back and forth between them. They were still clothed in the Japanese military uniform. "There's a reason we brought extra robes."

They both changed into their robes and left the uniforms hidden. The walk back through the woods was a long one, roughly three hours, and it got old real quick.

Once they had reached the village, the sun had burnt off all morning dew. They headed straight for Crowley's hut, knocked on the door, and quickly entered.

Across the way, a man stepped out of his hut and was quickly taken down with a quick snap of the neck. Skorn discretely dragged the body back into the hut and gently closed the door to remain unnoticed.

Inside the hut, Liam and Cathal took seats around the table. Crowley moved about with his normal worrisome pace throughout the hut and asked, "What's the news?"

Cathal explained to Crowley how they had encountered some dangerous situations several times before they had found the stone. Crowley seemed pleased with how they had handled themselves.

"So everything went fairly smooth," Crowley said, smiling. "I'm glad your ability to acquire both knowledge and skills is helping greatly. I was nervous about Liam going along."

"I didn't disappoint, Crowley. I promise," Liam added.

Cathal continued, "After we got the stone and made our way back to the cave's entrance, we were stopped by a mysterious man. It was very strange. He knew about me."

"What do you mean?" Crowley's eyes widened.

"He talked about my ordeal in Chicago and tried to physically overpower us and take the stone away."

Crowley wasn't happy. "I can't believe the Tarnen had already known about the dates and where you would be. This isn't good. Not good at all."

Crowley mumbled something they could barely hear; the only part they could hear was about some traitorous friend. "This man must be with the Tarnen. He must have been sent to stop you."

Cathal agreed. "He wanted the stone and knew I had it. His name was Skorn."

"I've never heard of such a name, but you shouldn't take this lightly at all. This changes things. If the Tarnen had sent him, then they must be very confident with his abilities. He should not be underestimated, and he is a very dangerous man, to say the least. I assume his ability is time travel," Crowley stated.

"He did overpower us, but we were able to get away with the stone. His combat skills are far superior to what I've seen or really read about. We had some other help. If it wasn't for this help, I don't think we would be having this conversation," Cathal replied.

Crowley was puzzled and said, "Who?"

"Gabriel," replied Cathal.

"You met Gabriel? Captain of the Outer Rim Guard?" Crowley's face grew pale.

"Yes, he was looking for Viktor. I told him I didn't know where he was. He also asked if I was part of Elluna's Guard, but I said I would ask you about Viktor. Are you part of the Guard?"

Crowley stepped closer to the table. "Yes, I am a member. You two are now honorary members as well for collecting these stones." Then he slammed his hands down on the table in frustration. "This is far worse than I thought. Gabriel would only be here if the Tarnen were truly coming. The Outer Rim Guard never leave their post unless this is true. It is the only absolute reason they would ever leave. Trust him. He is the leader."

Gabriel's reasons for showing up sent nerves rapidly throughout Cathal's body as he continued. "We do. He is scouting the Mongol's camp as we speak."

"You must go to him immediately. Don't waste time, and you must have no contact with anyone else. I fear this Skorn character is going to be playing a major role, the more you get involved," Crowley iterated.

Cathal replied, "I agree with you on Skorn. I definitely sensed someone spying on me at the library. I wonder if it was him."

"I wouldn't doubt it, especially if he can travel through time. He most surely must be the man the

Tarnen have sent to put an end to your quest. Be careful, both of you," Crowley said as he looked at both Liam and Cathal. They all said their good-byes, and Crowley wished them well on their way.

They started to head for the forest line, when Cathal stopped in his tracks. "Liam, go gather anything you need—food, water, anything. And meet me back here in one hour."

"What is going on?"

"I need to take care of one quick thing." Cathal ran off back into town, away from a confused Liam.

Cathal headed straight toward Keela's hut against Crowley's specific orders to leave immediately. With everything that had happened to him and with all that he thought would happen next, he needed to see her one last time.

Cathal quietly approached the open window, hoping not to be noticed by anyone inside. He peered through the window and saw no one. He looked in once more, hoping that the situation would change and that he would see his love, but the room inside was still empty. Disappointed, he decided that Crowley was right and that he needed to get moving.

Cathal turned around, and his mood drastically improved. Standing a few feet away from him, the angel now came running into his arms. Cathal and Keela embraced each other, kissing one another once and then twice; this continued for quite some time.

Keela stopped for a moment and then said, "I've missed you so."

Cathal smiled, closed his eyes, and began to squeeze her tightly as if he knew this was the last time he'd see her for a while, if ever again.

He opened his eyes and quickly leaned back. Through the crowd of people walking by behind her, he saw a face that he never wanted to see again—Skorn's face, staring straight at him with that now all-too-familiar devilish grin.

"Are you there? Everything all right?" Keela asked, staring into his eyes.

Cathal looked at Keela and quickly looked back to the crowd. The face was gone. Was he imagining things? Did Skorn really follow him back to Ireland?

"Cathal?" Keela said, beginning to worry. She began shaking him.

Quickly, he realized that he couldn't be without her any longer. Cathal snapped out of his daze, stared directly into Keela's eyes, and said, "I could get lost in your eyes forever and ever. Tonight, let's get married."

Keela smiled and began to laugh and then said, "Are you serious?"

Cathal nodded, smiling ear to ear.

Keela jumped once more into his arms and whispered into his ear, "Absolutely." She held him even tighter and began to kiss his ear, down to his neck.

Cathal smiled and said, "At sunset, meet me at the pond in the woods where we first kissed."

"All right." Keela let his hand go with a smile.

Cathal gently ran his fingers down Keela's smiling face and went in for one last kiss.

"See you soon," he said. Cathal looked back one last time as he ran off to meet Liam.

Liam lay on the grass, with his arms folded behind his head and his eyes closed. Cathal quietly crept up and kicked him lightly in the side. "Wake up!" Liam came to, startled, and hopped to his feet.

"Are we ready to go? I was just resting my eyes."

"We can't go anywhere yet," Cathal replied.

"What? What else do you have to do? Crowley said—"

Cathal interrupted, "I'm getting married to Keela tonight."

Liam's jaw dropped to the ground. "You're joking, right?"

"No, and I want you to perform the ceremony!"

"But Crowley said—"

"It'll be quick. I need to do this now. It can't wait." Cathal wasn't going to have it any other way, and Liam knew this.

Liam smiled and said, "Absolutely, tonight it is." They embraced in a congratulatory hug.

Liam and Cathal stood waiting at the edge of the pond. Slow ripples gently rode up against Cathal's toes as he stared out at his reflection.

"Think she's going to come?" Liam questioned.

"She will." Cathal still felt completely confused about everything that had happened—about Gabriel and the Tarnok and, more specifically, Skorn. Did he really see Skorn here in Ireland? Was he getting married to Keela with too much haste because of his vision of Skorn? These questions ran through his mind all day.

Footsteps from behind made them turn around quickly in surprise. Keela stood at the edge of the trees. The light from the moon shined down on her white dress, making her to look as bright as Gabriel did when they first met him, like an angel. Cathal always believed she was the most beautiful thing on this earth, and tonight he knew that to be true. Every feeling that he had ever had with her rushed through him. The butterflies in his stomach flooded to every part of his body, overwhelming him, causing him to tingle all over.

Keela stepped toward Cathal, smiling the whole way. "Are you ready?" she asked.

Cathal's vocals were paralyzed; he wasn't able to say anything. He just smiled back and held out his hand, which Keela placed in hers. They walked slowly to where Liam stood, back against the pond. The sun had gone down, but the lack of trees over the pond allowed the moon to illuminate the whole area. Keela's dress still shined bright.

They all went through the sacred ceremony, with Liam leading it. Liam went through the ceremony, with

Cathal and Keela both expressing their love and vows for each other.

"And now you may kiss your bride," Liam said to Cathal.

They embraced in their most memorable kiss of their lives. The sparks that filled Cathal's body made him weak.

"I'll let you two have the night to yourselves. See you in the morning." Liam looked at Cathal, who approved of what he said, and walked off, leaving them alone.

"Well, that's that, Husband," said Keela, her eyes staring straight into his.

Cathal smiled. "I never want this night to end."

They started to kiss and fell gracefully to the ground, and Cathal gently guided her down. They expressed their love for each other in ways they had never done before.

After they were done, Keela rolled over, her hand pressed on his chest. "What has been going on with you? You seem to disappear every now and again for long periods of time."

Cathal turned toward her and kissed her head, which now rested on his chest. "I love you. I promise you I will tell you when the time is right. You just need to trust me."

She nodded. "This is the happiest moment of my life." They both fell asleep underneath the night sky as Cathal wrapped himself around her, protecting her from the outside world. He hoped that he could always protect her, no matter what.

Hours later, birds jolted from the ground and hastily flew up into the sky. Footsteps became louder and faster. Cathal woke up and turned to see what was causing the commotion. He was completely stunned. He saw what he had hoped wasn't true—Skorn running straight for them.

CHAPTER FOURTEEN

"Wake up!" Cathal vigorously shook Keela. "What's going on?" Keela appeared startled as her eyes opened.

"No time to explain! Just run!" Cathal pulled her to her feet. He grabbed her hand, yanking her into a dash. Skorn was gaining ground.

Cathal and Keela sprinted through the woods, dodging many fallen branches and roots. "What are we running from?" shouted Keela.

Cathal turned his head to see where he was. Skorn was just several seconds behind. "There's a very bad man chasing us!" He pulled her hand closer to him to try to speed up the now frightened Keela.

Skorn moved through the woods at a swift pace; he avoided every root and branch as if he were racing on flat ground. The obstacles that had hindered their speed seemed to have no effect on him. He stared with vicious intent at Keela and Cathal.

Keela began to lose her footing. She had never moved this fast and hard in her life; her legs were on the verge of giving in and going limp. Cathal sensed this, so he started to craft obstacles for Skorn, hoping to slow him down. He threw back branches, pulled large rocks into the path, and changed directions several times. This did nothing to Skorn's speed; it seemed only to narrow the gap between them.

Cathal's speed drastically increased. He was no longer holding Keela's hand. He turned to see her screaming in pain on the ground. "Help!" she shouted.

He ran back over to her. Skorn was nearly a few yards away. Cathal picked her up and threw her over his shoulder and continued to run. Cathal's legs started to feel the impact of overexertion.

Keela screamed as she watched Skorn, who was now only a few feet away, dive for them. His hand grazed her head, ripping strands of her hair out, but he fell short of stopping them as he slammed to the ground.

Cathal had a momentary sigh of relief, but Keela screamed, "Keep going!" as she watched Skorn jump up and move with even more haste.

Cathal's legs got even heavier moving through thicker brush. He turned to see where Skorn was. This was a terrible mistake. Cathal no longer felt ground underneath him.

Keela flew from his shoulders as they both tumbled down the side of a cliff. They smashed into tree trunks, bushes, and roots as they continued rolling down until they hit the bottom about a hundred feet below. When they arrived at the bottom, Cathal and Keela both lay unconscious.

Skorn slowed down above as he saw them disappear. He crept to the edge of the cliff and peered over the edge to see the two bodies he was hunting battered, bruised, and still. His devilish grin emerged once more. "That was easier than I thought," he said. "My work is done." Skorn vanished into thin air.

CHAPTER FIFTEEN

Their two bodies lay battered and immobile several feet away from each other.

Cathal's eyes snapped open in sheer horror. He threw his chest upward. He frantically looked around in every direction, searching for Keela. He spotted her, unmoving.

"Oh no!" Cathal screamed as he crawled toward her body. Feeling was very minimal throughout his body as he struggled over to her. With all his strength, he lifted her into his arms. She wasn't breathing.

"Keela! Wake up!" He shook her vigorously. Adrenaline kicked in, and his strength reawakened inside. "Wake up!" Nothing helped. He began to smack her on the cheek to get some life back into her. Still nothing from her.

"Skorn! You will pay for this!" He belted out as he held her tight. Tears trickled down his face onto her as he rocked back and forth with her in his arms. Just last night she was wrapped in his arms for another reason. "How could I have been so stupid!" he thought. "I should have just listened to Crowley, and none of this would have happened!"

He began to focus on the bracelet. It began to glow. "If I went back in time, right before I decided to see Keela, Skorn would never know who she was," he thought. The glowing from the bracelet had faded. His body wasn't back with Liam yesterday before he decided to go see her. He still had her limp body in his arms. "No! Skorn, I will find you!" The scream stretched his entire vocal chords. He remembered Crowley specifically say that no matter what, he couldn't revisit a time that he had already lived.

Tears continued to flow down his face and onto hers. He closed his eyes, holding her tighter than before. He prayed to someone who would save her soul. Cathal stopped rocking and just held her. He didn't move or make a sound for a very long time.

Several hours later, still in the same position, Cathal felt his body move but not due to his own will. Keela's body began to twitch. She started to cough, which took him completely out of his terrible state. He was completely shocked.

"What happened?" Keela's eyes opened as she smiled at him.

Cathal's smile flooded his entire face. "How do you feel? I love you so much!"

"I feel great. I just got married to the love of my life, and I woke up in his arms."

"The fall must have wiped her memory clean of the recent chase. This is a good thing," he thought. "Keep her happy and not scared."

Keela closed her eyes again and, with a smile, stated, "I love you, Cathal." She went to sleep in his arms.

"Rest, my love." He kissed her on her forehead and lifted her up, holding her in his arms.

He made his way back to the village through the woods with her safe in his arms. Her father always went out hunting in the morning, so he would be safe bringing her back to her hut. The whole while, he continued to question what had happened just before. He told himself, "She was dead in my arms. How did she come back like that? What happened?" He was ashamed of what he did and knew Crowley could never find out, so he made sure to avoid him at all cost.

He entered the hut, brought her over to her bed, and placed her down gently. She opened her eyes. "Shh, you need rest," he whispered. "I'll be back later." He ran his fingers down her face once more and kissed her on the lips. "I love you now and forever," he added. All he got in response from her was a simple smile. That was all he wanted after what had just happened.

Cathal got up from the bed and left her hut, taking one last look at her before he left.

"Where have you been?" Liam questioned Cathal as he walked toward him at the edge of the forest line.

"I'll tell you on the way. We need to get moving," Cathal stated urgently.

After several hours into the woods, along the way back to their hiding spot for the stones, Cathal told him the whole story. Liam was completely amazed and terrified that Skorn was able to find them.

Their hiding spot for the stones hadn't changed one bit since they were last there. Cathal made sure of it by checking for the stones. "I'm so glad Skorn didn't find out about this place," he said.

Liam nodded. "We need to find him and take care of him."

"I agree. Hopefully Gabriel will be able to help us with that. Are we ready?" he asked Liam, and he nodded. Cathal grabbed Liam's arm and said, "To the Kingdom of Poland." The bright blue light engulfed them both, and they vanished.

CHAPTER SIXTEEN

New York City, USA—January 21, 1999

"What did I tell you?" Troy slammed both fists into his desk, causing some of the old wood to crack. "I specifically told you to go to Nanking and observe and nothing more!"

"It wasn't a total loss. I was—" Skorn tried to squeeze in an explanation but was stopped short by Troy's continuing rant.

"You weren't supposed to follow them back to Ireland either." Troy's veins in his forehead and hairline raised and began to pulsate around his temples. "Not only did you blow your cover completely, but also, you didn't kill them like you thought you did!"

A puzzled look rolled over Skorn's face. "That can't be. I chased them through the woods. Him and his girl.

I watched them fall to their deaths. I saw them lying on the ground, beaten to death."

Troy lifted his fists from the table, which left imprints in the wood. "Somehow they both survived the fall. And now, you went from being unknown to Cathal, to him knowing about you, hating you, and becoming prepared for you. Our best weapon was your stealth and a strike by you when it was the right time. Because of your idiotic actions, you've changed things for the worse."

Skorn's head lowered. "There is another problem."

"What is it?" Troy stared out to the night sky of the city, his veins still pumping.

"Cathal had help." He wanted to tell Troy the whole truth, but he was too afraid. "He had another person with him this time. His name was Liam. I think he is of family relation to Cathal."

"I think we really need to have The Six involved. You need to bring them with you. I've overestimated you, and apparently, you are unworthy to handle this yourself."

Skorn held back the other bit of information about the angelic creature, named Gabriel, helping them as well. He felt Troy would surely make him bring The Six with him. This was Skorn's task and his alone, Skorn thought. "No, please…let me handle this myself," Skorn said.

Troy continued to stare out the window, puffing on his cigar.

"Can't I go back and finish the job?" Skorn pleaded with him.

"No, you need to get back on task," Troy insisted.

"But!" Skorn angrily protested.

"Skorn! You see what happens when you don't do what I ask. Things go awry. I know what needs to be done. Now go to the Kingdom of Poland. He will be there. The Mongolian army is protecting the Fire Stone. Just observe, and let them handle Cathal and this other boy, Liam."

"Can we move the stones that are still protected by the Tarnen?" asked Skorn.

Troy waited in silence for a brief moment, contemplating the idea, which, in any other circumstance, would be completely foolish. Cathal, however, had proven to be a worthy adversary. "No, that isn't the way it's supposed to be," Troy said eventually. "They've been spread apart for a reason. It is safer this way. It would be too easy for him if they were all together. Cathal has been crafty acquiring two of the stones. But have faith in what the Tarnen have set up. Once they were given to each of the groups, they were told to kill anyone who tried to take the stones. This would even include you, just in case you were turned by Elluna's Guard. They would defend it with their lives."

"I respectfully disagree, but I will do as I am ordered to," Skorn answered.

Troy calmly made his way toward his chair, sat down, and sighed. "Go to the Mongols. They will be looking for you now, and observe them unseen, and if the opportunity presents itself, kill both Cathal and Liam."

Skorn smirked. "At least I am able to finish the job I started," he thought. He had never botched up a kill until now. This bothered him to no end. "Finally, it will be done. Thank you," said Skorn, and then he vanished into thin air.

Troy stood up and walked over to one of the bookshelves. His eyes scrolled through book spine after book spine until they stopped at a particularly ancient-looking one. He pulled it out and walked back over to the desk. He blew the dust off the cover, opened it to a specific page, and began to read.

CHAPTER SEVENTEEN

Outskirts of Legnica—April 9, 1241

The ground rumbled. Hooves pounded into the grass, moving faster and faster toward their targets. A group of European knights on horseback with bright silver-plate armor chased after the Mongolian invaders as they began to get pulled away from their own army.

The Mongols shifted directions, turning toward their left. Their bows were now aimed at their pursuers who were in plate mail. The archers fired at will, moving at full speed on horseback. Horses and knights began to drop one by one. Arrows struck the knights between their armor, hitting their necks and faces, sending them backward and right off their horses. Horses fell to the ground, bringing their riders with them into a stampede. It was a complete massacre of the European knights.

Cathal and Liam watched this safely above on a hill, behind all the bloodshed. "Can't these knights see they are helpless against this kind of attack?" Liam asked, awestruck.

"An amazing tactic, I must say," Gabriel said as he landed just feet away from them as they stared out over the battle. "The Mongols feign their retreat, detach the knights from their main body, and take them out one by one."

Another round of feigning by the Mongols occurred, while they stood there and watched. Thousands of arrows flew through the air, clouding the knights from view. Another round destroyed men, and their death was by arrow.

"This is true," said Cathal. "The Mongols do destroy the European troops on this day. I read about this battle, but to see it in person, the books don't do it justice. There's a sea of horses on both sides." Cathal felt admiration for the events he had read about taking place before his very eyes.

"Let's get to the important matter, shall we?" Gabriel interrupted Cathal's thought.

"Right, the stone, do you know where it is?" Cathal asked.

Gabriel pointed down toward the back of a group of Mongols, impatiently waiting to get their chance to get involved in the battle. "Do you see that one soldier with the extra sack hanging from his horse?" he asked.

"How can you tell that sack has the stone?" Liam asked.

"How'd I know you two had a stone before in China?" Gabriel smiled and looked at Liam. "I can sense these things. I sense it in that area, and that soldier is the only one that has extra equipment. It has to be him."

"So what now? How do we get that stone away from him? There must be hundreds of men around him. You saw what they did to those knights. This seems impossible with just the three of us," Liam stated.

Cathal stared out at the massacre before him. Mongolian soldiers were now off their horses, cutting the right ears off the dead. He had read that this was how they counted their casualties—by the number of right ears taken.

Gabriel smiled and said, "I can cause a diversion!"

Liam and Cathal seemed confused but waited for Gabriel to continue.

Gabriel began to pace back and forth, staring at the ground. "I can pull that whole group of archers to chase me. Everyone will be focused on taking me down. Then you can slip right in with them, as I distract them, and steal the stone from him."

"Do you see their accuracy? One of them will hit you," Liam answered with concern.

Gabriel broke out into laughter. "I'm too fast. Even if one happened to hit me, which it won't, their arrows are no match for my body. They will not pierce my skin."

"That's great and all, but how are we going to keep up with everyone on foot?" Cathal asked.

"Look over there, we can use them." Liam pointed over past the group of men toward two horses, alone near the forest line. A few feet away, two soldiers entered the woods.

"Good catch, Liam. This is our opportunity. Take them out, and get into their gear to join their ranks," Gabriel demanded. And then he picked them both up, one in each arm, and flew toward the horses, giving them no time to reconsider his quickly formulated plan.

From the time they were picked up to the time Gabriel dropped them off hundreds of yards away, mere seconds passed. They had no time to react. It was as if they were literally teleported from one spot to another. Cathal saw that Gabriel really could move as fast as he wanted.

The drop of the two boys startled the horses but not enough to cause a commotion. "I'll wait until I see you two move into position," Gabriel said and then disappeared into the sky. The two soldiers were now so deep into the woods that they couldn't be seen from where Liam and Cathal now stood.

They quietly crept past the horses to the forest line and could now hear the voices of the two Mongols. They were speaking in their native tongue. Cathal knew they were talking about women they had come in contact with in previous villages. Cathal looked disgusted.

Both men were leaning up against different trees, urinating on the trunks below. Cathal and Liam quietly maneuvered around bushes and trees toward them. Any sound they made were muffled by their urinating. Carefully, they tiptoed right behind them and slammed their heads into the trees in front of them; the two soldiers both fell over unconscious.

They quickly changed into their victims' armor. Liam seemed to enjoy this and said, "This time, I'm not a prisoner." Cathal just shook his head and laughed. The armor from the soldiers was light and flexible, made from hardened leather and iron. The Mongols were nomadic and relied on a quick attack, so they wore light armor.

The horses seemed irritated at their presence. It was as if they knew that underneath the armor, Cathal and Liam were not their normal riders. Liam took a step back. "Wait," Cathal warned Liam as he went up to the two horses and calmly started to whisper to them, stroking their manes. With every stroke and word uttered by Cathal, the horses became less irritable and more controllable. "Good, that's it. It's safe now," Cathal said to Liam.

Liam stepped over to his horse, as if not to cause any alarm, and gently hopped up on the saddle. "I really need to go to this library," he said jokingly.

Cathal laughed as he jumped on top of his horse and replied, "Maybe when we have time."

"I still don't understand if we can travel through time. How you can say 'When we have time'? We have all the time in the world."

Cathal looked peeved at this response.

"No more talking when we get up there. We don't want to be singled out. Keep silent until we get the sign," Cathal stated.

They rode their horses back to the large group, positioning themselves close to the man with the stone.

The smell of the area was completely rank. It seemed as though the people had apparently not cleaned themselves for days, weeks, or even months at a time. Horses relieved themselves right where they stood. It took all their will to pretend they were used to it. The archers around them were becoming impatient, watching their fellow men slaughter the knights. They wanted to get in on the action.

Cathal and Liam kept their heads down but would peer up every now and then to keep their eye on the man with the sack; the man was not five feet in front of them, and he kept touching it to make sure it was there. "That has to be it—he is more focused on that sack than the actual battle," whispered Liam, and Cathal agreed.

They watched as another round of archers pulled the knights away. The European knights were a mix of Poles, Czechs, and Germans that were sent to put a halt to the Mongolian invasion but were almost decimated to this point. The Mongolian men in front of them began to cheer when they were interrupted with a loud crack. Cathal saw a flash of light and a huge explosion nearby. Men and horses were sent flying back. Everyone was confused. They had no idea where the explosion had come from, and then there was another loud crack, and more men reeled into the air.

"I'm up here!" Gabriel waved to the archers, taunting the Mongols and laughing at them. Angered by this, they began to fire at Gabriel, who continually dodged all their arrows. He moved with such haste that there were some points in the episode when you couldn't see him at all and others when he would reappear to taunt the soldiers again. More and more arrows continued to miss him.

Every Mongol in the back of the army was firing at him except for the man with the stone. He kept a tight hold on that sack. Cathal and Liam moved a little closer to him, now within an arm's reach. Gabriel shot down another lightning bolt, sending more men into the air.

When Gabriel had drawn the focus of the soldiers, he started to fly away, pulling the archers with him through taunts and attacks. The man with the stone followed as well. "No! He's moving with them!" Liam called out.

The man heard this and rapidly turned his head, making eye contact with Liam. Alarmed, he maneuvered himself away from them and into the crowd of charging horses. "We've got to follow him!" Cathal ordered.

Arrows continued to fly through the air and miss Gabriel as he pulled more archers away from their main body, similar to what they had done to the European knights. The rest of the Mongols didn't seem to notice because they were focused on the defeated knights in front of them. Cathal and Liam continued to pursue the man through the stampede of horses, but he had disappeared. They couldn't find him. They had lost him.

Out of nowhere, a man jumped from his horse onto the back of Liam and began to strangle him. Liam fought back and head-butted him, causing him to let go and fall off. "They know we aren't one of them!" he shouted.

Cathal shot an arrow at one who came at him. Out of the corner of his eyes, he saw one lone man on horseback galloping away from the stampede and into the woods. "Liam! I've spotted him. He's left the group and is headed for the forest. I'm going to go after him! You stay with Gabriel!"

Liam nodded as he continued to take down archers firing at himself and Gabriel.

Cathal slowed down and made a right cut across several archers before dashing for the woods. Huge flashes of light from Gabriel appeared brighter throughout the sky as the sun fell below the tree line, while Cathal gained ground on the rider, who was almost clear into the woods.

As the man holding the sack disappeared into the forest, Cathal entered a little less than ten seconds later. He slowly came to a walking pace and moved in quietly, still on horseback. With the sun setting and the trees overtop blocking out what was left of the light, the place was very dark and hard for Cathal to see in.

He continued to move through the forest, peering in all directions, looking for any sign of the rider or the stone. He saw nothing. It was as if the rider and his horse had vanished into thin air.

Cathal made his way past a specific tree and heard a crack from above. Quickly, he glanced up and saw the man crashing down upon him, knocking him off his horse to the ground. Cathal lay unconscious as the man picked him up and lifted him over his shoulder.

CHAPTER EIGHTEEN

A burst of light flashed in the middle of a field and brightened the night sky. Skorn arose from a kneeled position. He heard the faint sound of men celebrating over a hill to his left. He made his way up the hill to see an encampment of troops, celebrating a recent victory. "Perfect," Skorn thought.

He wasted no time and headed straight for the tents. No stealthy sneaking in and no studying of the camp first this time. About twenty yards from the edge of the camp, two men spotted him and said, "Stop! Who goes there?" The men were dressed in leather, each holding a circular shield in one hand and a spear in the other.

Skorn raised his hands and stopped. "I come in peace. I have valuable information, and I wish to share it with your leader."

The two warriors moved toward Skorn cautiously. One began to pat him down to check for weapons, while the other held a spear pressing directly into his neck. "You have peculiar clothes," the man holding the spear stated, looking at his jeans and hooded sweatshirt.

"Aye," responded Skorn.

"Come," said the man. One warrior moved in front of Skorn, while the other moved behind him, his spear poking Skorn's back in case he tried to do something foolish. The camp was alive with celebration. Fires were lit, and men were drinking, cheering, and dancing all around. These men were larger than the average man, but Skorn didn't seem intimidated at all. He just smiled as he pushed through the camp, similar to a prisoner of war.

They stopped at a tent much grander than the rest. One of the warriors entered the tent. The spear pressed a little harder into his back. "I've got an itch. Could you press a little harder?" Skorn said this, turned his head, and smiled at the man. Insulted, the man pushed a little more, piercing the skin. Skorn felt blood drip down his back and said, "That's better."

The same warrior who walked him through the encampment emerged from the tent and said, "You can come and explain yourself to our earl."

Skorn entered the tent. An even larger man lay with a woman on top of him. He tossed the woman to the side, and she quickly covered herself up. The man sat upright and said, "I am Valdi." Then he began to dress himself and said, "I am the earl of this clan. You interrupted my celebrating. This had better be worth my time."

"My name is Skorn. It's a pleasure to have an audience with you, Earl Valdi. I have some information for you. I know of a village that has great wealth to be claimed."

Valdi's eyes widened with curiosity. "I am a very wealthy man already, but I always have a thirst for more."

Valdi smiled.

"I can take you to this village, but I need a favor from you in return," Skorn replied.

"How do I know I can trust you?" Valdi stood up and walked over to an open chest in the corner of the room. He placed his hand deep in the chest, pulling out many coins and small golden trinkets before slowly releasing them back into the pile.

"I have many spoils," said Valdi. "Why would I risk them for you? You come out of nowhere with this information for me. I neither know you nor have ever heard of you, and you're dressed in things I have never seen. And I've been all around the world."

Irritation flowed through Valdi's words.

"Please, I am telling the truth. Let me challenge your best fighter. If I win, will you then take me up on my offer?" Skorn smirked.

"Ha-ha! I would love to see this. You're just a puny little boy! Yes, I will take you up on your offer." Valdi made eye contact with the warrior at the entrance. "Call on Dolfri." The warrior quickly disappeared with his orders.

"To the death?" Skorn asked.

"Aye! To the death!" Valdi laughed.

Skorn, Valdi, and his personal guard left the tent and strode toward the center of the military camp. Loud screams and cheers began to erupt, and they got louder as they approached a crowded mass of warriors chanting, "Dolfri, Dolfri, Dolfri!"

Valdi shoved Skorn through an opening in the crowd. The drunken celebratory warriors created a large circle surrounding Skorn, still chanting Dolfri's name. He peered through the crowds and saw no one coming forward. Then through bodies being shoved aside, a much larger figure emerged from the center of the crowd.

Dolfri pushed aside the remaining warriors at the circle's edge. He towered over the already large crowd of chanting men. In his right hand, resting over his shoulder, he held a huge two-handed battle-ax. Skorn guessed that it must have been the full length of his own body.

A warrior tossed a one-handed sword toward Skorn's feet. He picked up the small sword, which was about the same length as Dolfri's ax hilt. Dolfri smiled and stomped toward Skorn. The ground shook right underneath Skorn with every step he made. Skorn hid the hint of fear he had inside and walked up to Dolfri. They stopped just one foot from each other. He could smell the rank breath of Dolfri filling his nose. Skorn tilted his head upward, looking straight into the eyes of Dolfri, who looked downward toward Skorn. He towered practically two feet over Skorn.

Dolfri grabbed Skorn by the neck with his left hand and lifted him straight off the ground to his eye level. Skorn's legs kicked at Dolfri's body but had no effect on Dolfri. Dolfri threw him backward, sending him into the crowd and knocking over several warriors in his path.

Skorn giggled as he picked himself up off the ground and grabbed his miniscule sword in his right hand. "So that's how we are going to play," he said. He sprinted toward the giant in the middle of the opening. Dolfri prepped his first swing with the giant ax, but Skorn moved faster than any of them had ever seen, and before Dolfri could connect with him, Skorn sliced Dolfri's right arm clear off his body, sending the ax with it.

Dolfri, in shock, looked down at what once was his immensely strong arm now a nub just below the elbow and spilling out blood onto the ground. The crowd went absolutely silent from pure shock. The only sound came from Skorn throwing his sword to the ground.

"Let's make this a fair fight!" Skorn snickered as he placed one arm behind his back and taunted Dolfri. Dolfri exploded with rage and charged straight for him. Skorn dodged him as Dolfri tripped to the ground, falling toward him. Skorn pounced on top of him and pounded both of his fists into Dolfri's face until he was unconscious.

Skorn stood up and strutted over to Dolfri's ax and picked it up. He walked back over to Dolfri's unmoving body, dragging the ax, and looked at Valdi for approval. Ashamed, Valdi nodded. Skorn struggled a little to lift the ax and then sent it crashing down over Dolfri's neck, slicing right through and ending the giant's life.

Skorn dropped Dolfri's ax and strutted, with his head held high, back to Valdi's tent, followed by Valdi's personal guard. The crowd stayed unequivocally silent; everyone stared at either Skorn or the headless body of their most beloved warrior. Every warrior backed out of Skorn's way as if he were the plague. Skorn loved this; he loved being feared, most of all.

Back in the tent, Skorn sat down at the main table with Valdi at the other end.

"Tell me, Skorn, where is this village you speak of?" Valdi asked. His confident aura from before the fight had faded and was replaced with fear. Skorn now had the upper hand.

Skorn's all-too-familiar devious smirk reappeared. "I know of a village to the north. If you raid this village and take its treasures, you will have tenfold what you already have acquired."

He knew this was a lie, but for his intentions, he needed to entice them.

"Why are you telling me this? Do you have something against these people?"

"I have a personal quarrel with some specific people who live there. I want to deal with them on my own."

"What about everyone and everything else?" Valdi questioned.

"You can do whatever you like. Plunder, burn, ravage, and kill—whatever you and your men desire." Skorn sneered.

"Let's be on our way!" Valdi laughed.

CHAPTER NINETEEN

Cathal awoke, and he found that he could barely move. Ropes bound his arms and he realized quickly he was bound to a tree trunk. He attempted to maneuver his hands free from the ropes, but they were tied so tightly that he was losing a lot of circulation.

"Tell me"—a Mongolian soldier emerged from behind the tree and stepped directly in front of Cathal—"why were you chasing me away from the battle?"

Cathal pretended he didn't speak his language as he attempted to move his weak hands through the knots.

Aggravated, the man took out a knife and stabbed Cathal, piercing his left arm. He winced in pain: it was the same arm he had injured in Chicago. "I know you understand me, and I know you speak my tongue," the man insisted.

Cathal shook his head. The man pressed the knife deeper into his arm.

"I think we got off on the wrong foot." The man pulled the knife out of Cathal's arm. The Mongolian soldier continued. "My name is Chuluun. I am of high rank in our horde. What is your name?"

Cathal wasn't getting any closer with loosening the knot. A cold feeling crawled over his hands as he started to lose more circulation. He needed to stall for time, and he hoped maybe Liam or Gabriel would come looking for him. He hoped. These guys he was dealing with weren't the type of people to leave unwanted people alive. He needed to keep this soldier talking to distract him and give him some information.

"My name is Cathal."

"And what is so special about me, Cathal? Why'd you continue to pursue me?"

"I...um...I wanted your horse. I'd been jealous from the start. You know, mine rarely would do what I had wanted, and yours seemed to."

"You're lying!" Chuluun punched Cathal in the face, and blood splattered on a tree not far from where they were. Cathal's hands began to burn.

"You wanted the stone, didn't you?" Chuluun shouted as he jammed his finger into Cathal's wound. This caused Cathal to cringe in excruciating pain. "Who sent you? How did you know I had it?"

Chuluun dug his finger deeper and twisted.

Cathal screamed out in pain. The smell of burning rope drifted into Cathal's nose. Chuluun laughed and taunted Cathal. "Too bad you're going to die knowing that you failed!"

Then the strangest thing happened: Cathal stopped trying to break free of the ropes. Tension had left his shoulders, and he felt no restriction in his hands. He was free.

He wasted no time and immediately surprised Chuluun with a right upper cut, sending him backward and onto the ground. He had no idea how the rope knots were gone; the only thing he was concerned with was the stone.

Chuluun hopped to his feet and chuckled. "Interesting," he said. Cathal sprinted toward him, and Chuluun immediately vanished, stopping Cathal abruptly in his tracks.

"Huh, what the—" Cathal's head knocked back rapidly as if he were punched in the face by an invisible being.

"I underestimated you, Cathal. Too bad you underestimated me as well," said a voice, echoing in the woods.

Cathal now turned his view rapidly in all directions, trying to pinpoint where this invisible man was, preparing himself for an attack from any direction.

Footsteps quickly came from his left side, but Cathal was too late. A force slammed into his wounded arm, sending him flying into the air, and he cracked his ribs, as he crashed onto some thick roots below him.

Cathal lay helpless on the ground, wounded and in pain. He pressed down on his ribs and tried to dull the pain.

"Cathal! Are you all right?" Liam called out as he rushed toward him.

Cathal urgently motioned for Liam to get away from there before the invisible man saw him, but it was too late.

Liam stopped, and his eyes widened in sheer horror. His hands rushed to his neck, fighting an unseen grip, which had been crushing him there. Still fighting, his legs began to swing back and forth. Liam was now floating, or so it appeared to Cathal.

Liam continued to struggle, pulling away at the invisible grip and staring at Cathal, who was now crawling toward him. Liam's struggling ceased; his body went limp, and he fell into a puddle of mud, which splattered mud all around. This last fact, however, proved a blessing in disguise for Cathal: the mud had splattered all over the invisible man, forming almost what looked like a human shape. Enraged at the helpless feeling he had and at the Mongol attack on Liam, Cathal, for some reason, miraculously began to heal himself. The cracked and swelling ribs and the pain went away, and the knife wound on his arm hurt no more.

Cathal stood up and stared at the specks of mud floating in the air and dashed straight for the now visible figure, spearing the person into the muddy puddle. More of the figure began to take shape as Cathal sat on top of him, punching him back and forth. His fists repeatedly connected with Chuluun's face. As he continued to beat him down, the Mongol's invisibility began to wear off, and his face reappeared again, now bloody and beaten.

Cathal stopped and stood up, staring over the unconscious body and looking for the stone on it, but he couldn't see it.

Within a brief moment, Cathal fell backward as the man swept him with his leg.

"No more games!" Chuluun screamed as he stood over Cathal.

He lifted Cathal and hurled his body at a tree, his back and head smashing against the trunk. He fell to the ground.

Cathal was now in more agonizing pain than before. He began to feel extremely light-headed. His vision blurred; the back of his head felt cold and wet. He reached to feel the back of his head and touched a wet substance. When he brought his hand in view, it was covered in blood.

Cathal could barely make out what he saw due to the blurriness of his vision, but he could see the Mongolian soldier bend over, pick something up, and start walking toward him.

"No more questions, no more fighting. You're not getting the stone. Whatever quest you were on shall die right here." Chuluun gave his ultimatum.

The man, now standing over the helpless Cathal, raised his sword. Cathal closed his eyes and tried one last attempt to sweep his legs, but before he could do so, there was a loud thud, and Chuluun fell to the ground, knocked out from behind.

Liam stood over Cathal, holding a large tree branch. He dropped the branch and his arms. To Cathal, he looked exhausted. He made his way over to Cathal, grabbed his hand, and helped him up.

Cathal's vision came back into focus. He placed his hand on the back of his head but couldn't find a cut anymore. "Hmm, really strange…"

They made their way over to the motionless body and patted it down, looking for the stone or the sack it was in. They found nothing.

"Could it have been on his horse still?" Liam questioned.

Cathal nodded, smiled, and whistled. Within moments, the man's horse came galloping out of the darkened woods, right up to Cathal, and rubbed his nose into his chest.

"There, boy, do you have something for me?" Cathal brushed the beautiful dark brown horse's hair, while he reached around for the sack hanging from the saddle. "This has to be it."

Cathal unhooked the sack from the saddle and brought it to the muddy ground. Liam peered over his shoulder as Cathal opened the top of the bag and placed his hands inside. In a second, he pulled out another beautifully obsidian stone.

They studied the stone; there were several wavy lines resembling the flames of fire. "It must be Fire," Liam stated in wonderment.

A groaning sound arose in the air from behind them. They both quickly turned around to see the Mongol standing there, dazed and confused. *Whack!* He fell to the ground again. Gabriel smiled from behind him and said, "Well, that was easy! We need two more."

"Yes, we've got Earth, Water, and Fire. We need Air, and Viktor's center stone to join them all," Cathal answered.

"Where to?" Liam smiled excitedly.

"To Nazi Germany," Cathal replied and sighed.

"You boys better rest up," Gabriel warned. "I've seen what they are capable of. You're both going to need all your strength there."

"You're right," suggested Liam. "We should head back to our village for some good rest."

Cathal immediately shot down Liam's suggestion. "I wouldn't go back to the village. Not after Skorn followed us back there. It's too dangerous, and we don't know who else could be watching us. Let's head back to drop the stone in our hiding spot and rest up there."

"I will scout out Germany, while you get back your energy. The date is June 5, 1944, right?" Gabriel asked.

Cathal nodded in shock that he knew. Gabriel smiled and took off into the sky.

"He must have read your mind, ha-ha!" Liam joked.

Cathal smiled, grabbed Liam's arm, and said, "Ready." Their bodies glowed of bright blue, and then they disappeared.

When they got back to the woods, Cathal placed the Fire Stone with the other two stones in the hiding spot, while Liam made a fire. Liam made Cathal tell him about Nazi Germany to help prepare him for what might befall them as they fell asleep by the hot fire. The smoke of the fire smelled much stronger this time, more than a normal fire usually did.

The next morning, before sunrise, they both awoke and gathered their things to teleport to their next destination.

"Here we go!" Cathal shouted as they disappeared once again.

CHAPTER TWENTY

"This sure is some good deer," Keela said to her father while they sat enjoying his latest hunt in the forest.

"Thank you. You know, Keela…" Aidan paused in his response.

"What is it, Pa?" Keela responded, rubbing the cross on a necklace on her neck. Cathal had given it to her a long time ago.

"He gave that to you, the boy Cathal?" Aidan asked.

She smiled and took her hand off the cross. "Yes, he did."

"You should bring him over sometime." He squeezed out the statement in between stuffing his face with his meal.

"What did you say?" Keela was confused but happy at the same time. This was something she never thought she would ever hear from her father.

"I said you can invite him over sometime. I never really gave him a chance. I always felt he involved himself in dangerous adventures, which I wanted you to have no part in. I'm under the assumption I'm just going to have to accept that you are becoming a lady now, and there will be men trying to court you."

Keela hopped up from her chair and ran over to him, hugging him more firmly than she had in a very long time.

"Whoa! Easy, child. I didn't say I liked him yet!" He laughed, trying to get out of the grip of her arms.

"But still, you're willing to meet him! Thank you, Pa!" Keela wouldn't let go.

"Ahhhh!" Some screams and shouts coming from outside their hut put an end to their embrace.

Keela and Aidan rushed to the door. Keela poked her head out, and Aidan pulled it back in just as fast. "Let me look!" he demanded. "I don't want them spotting you!"

Aidan peered through the cracks of his door. Keela could partially see what was going on outside.

Outside, villagers, screaming, ran for their lives as large men with spears, swords, and shields swept through the village and attacked them. All around, the men were cutting down defenseless people and stripping them of all their possessions. He could hear screaming from inside the huts as these raiders ran out with precious belongings, taking whatever they pleased.

Aidan grabbed an ax. "Stay inside and hide!" He hugged Keela just as hard as she had, before saying, "I love you!"

As fast as Keela tried to stop him, he was gone. She began to tear up but did as her father had ordered and hid underneath a bunch of deer fur blankets, which had been made from Aidan's game-hunting prizes.

Outside the tent, large men were antagonizing Lassi, an elderly woman who lived not far from Aidan and Keela. Aidan lunged for the invader, raising his ax to swing, but the ax never touched the man, and Aidan never got the swing off. This was because a spear pierced his back and pushed right through his heart and out his chest. Aidan stopped immediately and dropped the ax.

Valdi pulled the spear right out of Aidan's lifeless body as he fell to the ground.

"Remember, you can take all you want except for whom we agreed upon!" Skorn reminded the earl of the Vikings.

Valdi nodded as he continued his pillaging and signaled his Viking clan to do the same.

Crowley saw Aidan lying on the ground from afar and came running over to Skorn, sword in hand.

"You'll never stop him!" Crowley screamed as he swung at Skorn from behind.

"What did you say?" Skorn replied, quickly parrying his attack, and stood defensively toward Crowley.

Valdi then came from the side, swinging at Crowley, who countered with his sword and a blow to Valdi's stomach, which broke through his armor.

"He's mine, Valdi! Move along!" Skorn ordered the larger man as he ran off.

Crowley wasted no time in going back after Skorn. Back and forth they went. One swung, and the other blocked. Their skills were very evenly matched.

"And who might you be?" Skorn smiled as he blocked another blow.

"I am called Crowley, and I'm the one who will put an end to this!" He parried one of Skorn's incoming attacks.

"Listen, old man, you've got some skills, but this will not end well for you!" Skorn laughed as he began to toy with Crowley, not even blocking his attacks now but merely dodging the swings of Crowley's sword.

"I may be old, but as long as I live, I won't let you hurt him! He's going to find all the stones, and the Tarnok's plan will be thwarted. They will never rule!" Crowley replied.

Skorn continued to laugh. "I'm not here for him. And he's not going to acquire all the stones. I'm here to take away his main motivation!"

Crowley and Skorn continued to match each other's blows.

Those words repeated in Crowley's head as he kept fighting Skorn: "I'm here to take away his main motivation." Crowley then realized that this whole raid wasn't for Cathal but purely for Keela. "She's innocent!" Crowley shouted at Skorn.

Crowley began to fight with a ferocity that faltered Skorn. Skorn was losing his ability to dodge Crowley's attacks, who seemed to be connecting more and more. Skorn's movements and attacks slowed down.

"She's the reason Cathal continues on. Take her out of the picture, and he has nothing! No motivation! That will break him!" Skorn explained part of his devious plans.

The words that came out of Skorn's mouth only seemed to enrage Crowley even more. He began to fight with the ability of a man half his age and twice his strength. Skorn was overpowered and fell back to the ground.

Crowley stood over Skorn and lifted his sword. "Your part is over!" Crowley screamed as he threw his sword down toward Skorn.

Skorn quickly kicked Crowley's leg, staggering him and interrupting his swing. He grabbed his own sword and thrust it up into the chest of Crowley and twisted.

Skorn got to his feet, still holding the sword and keeping Crowley upright. He moved in close to him and whispered in his ear, "No, old man, your part is done. I'll kill Keela, kill Cathal, and then the Tarnok will finally rule this world."

Skorn pushed Crowley over, removing his sword from his lifeless body.

The raid continued as villagers continued to scream and as the large Vikings continued to defile. The invading Vikings ravaged, beat, and took the lives of most in the village, and many of the huts were set ablaze when they couldn't find any other useful items inside.

A terrified Keela continued to hide under the fur, hearing all the anarchy around her. She listened as a man entered the hut. She prayed it was her father but realized quickly, by the sounds the man coming inside made, that it wasn't him but one of the savage intruders. A knife landing in her vision through the cracks between the hides confirmed this fact. She reached for it and pulled it tightly to her side underneath the fur. Footsteps drew closer to her body and stopped.

Her heart skipped several beats. She could hear the man's grotesque breathing not too far away, which abruptly came to a sudden stop. Everything went silent. Keela wondered if he had spotted her. Her heart stopped, and she froze completely down to every thought. Not one sound registered in her mind, not even the screams outside. The brief seconds after felt like an eternity. His feet didn't move or make a sound. If he had found her, what was he waiting for?

And then the sound of footsteps started to drift to the other side of the hut. Keela knew this was her only chance. She stood up, throwing the hides off her. The Viking had his back to her, smelling her clothes from her chest. Keela jumped toward him with her knife outstretched to stab him on impact.

It was too late. The Viking spun around, grabbing her wrist, squeezing it so tightly that her hand opened right up. The knife, her only protection, fell right to the floor.

"Pity, you look like the one he wants, and I could have had you all to myself!" The man stared at her. Keela could just sense his impure thoughts. Her only reaction was to scream until nothing came out anymore.

"Maybe I can have a little fun before I bring you to him!" He slammed her to the table. Keela fought with every ounce of her life, smacking and clawing; she even ripped off a chunk of skin from his face. This only seemed to fuel his craving for her. "This won't be over quickly. Fighting will do you no good!" the Viking yelled.

Keela closed her eyes, and she tried to imagine being with Cathal somewhere else, because she didn't want her last vision to be of this evil monster doing this heinous act.

Blood splattered across her face, and all the weight of the man came crashing down on her.

Skorn pulled him off her. "You are my prize!" He lifted her up over his shoulder and left the hut. Keela looked back and saw the man's throat had been sliced right open.

Keela had left one nightmare and entered another.

"Let go of me! My father will get you! My love, Cathal, will get you!" Keela shouted. She still had some fight in her hanging over his shoulders, trying to wiggle free.

Skorn had thrown her to the ground and bent down over her. "I don't think your father's alive anymore, sweetie, and I hope Cathal does come!"

Skorn punched her in the face, knocking her unconscious.

Keela awoke, tied to a post. The village was desolate and silent; the sounds of screams and weapons clanking were no more. Ash and smoke ascended from the huts that were still left partially standing. Skorn stood next to a fire, holding his sword in it.

"Ah, you're awake. I've been waiting for that or Cathal to come. Still no sign of your love." Skorn smiled.

"He'll come!" Keela's energy was fading in and out.

Skorn started to pile up hay and sticks and snugged it underneath her feet. Keela screamed out Cathal's name with a resurgence of energy.

"Good! I want you to scream! I want him to hear you call out and not be able to do anything!"

She continued to scream, but then she lost the energy again. Skorn walked up to her and pulled the necklace off her chest. "Did he give this to you?"

She spit right in his face. The cross fell from his grasp, landing safely back on her chest.

He brushed his face with his forearm, wiping off Keela's spit. "I guess so."

Skorn went over to the fire and grabbed a torch from it. "Well, I'm not going to take it from you. I want you to have something remaining on your corpse to let him know that it was you who burned alive right here!" And after a moment, he added, "And that your last moments on earth were not of peace and happiness but of pure pain and suffering!" Skorn threw the torch into the hay underneath her, which set ablaze to the hay below her feet.

Skorn walked away smiling as Keela continued to scream out Cathal's name as the fire began to burn at her feet.

CHAPTER TWENTY-ONE

Berlin, Germany—June 5, 1944

Cathal and Liam appeared immediately after the flash of blue light faded in the night sky. Cathal quickly pulled Liam down to the ground, covering themselves in the brush of the fields.

"Where is it? I don't see any Nazis." said Liam.

"It's in a bunker. Somewhere in this field is a secret Nazi base hidden underground."

Liam began to speak but Cathal interrupted.

"Quiet, while I scout the area."

Cathal raised his head slightly over the thick brush to survey the area around him. He had an eerie feeling about the situation. He hadn't seen or felt Gabriel's presence. "He should be here where the stone is," he thought.

Explosions from the nearby city brightened the night sky and shook the ground where they hid. "Bombers," Cathal answered Liam's question before he could even ask it. "We need to find the entrance. Follow my lead."

Cathal got down into a horizontal position and began to crawl uphill through the thick grass. Moving one arm at a time to stay unnoticed to everything around, Liam followed verbatim.

They continued to move up a small hill, pushing through the grass and moving ever so slowly forward. They finally came to a point where the dirt and grass met with concrete. He stopped.

"Hold on," Cathal said. He slid further up onto the concrete and poked his head over the edge. They were directly above the entrance to a bunker. From his view, there was no sign of any guards. His plan to knock out a guard and take his uniform was foiled. He would have to enter a Nazi base with tenth-century robes on.

If not meeting up with Gabriel right away didn't freak Cathal out, this certainly did—an unguarded entrance to a Nazi bunker in the middle of World War II.

"You need to stay here until I tell you to move," Cathal demanded.

"But it's not safe here," Liam whispered in panic. "You need me, but more importantly, I need you."

"Trust me. Something isn't right, and if something goes wrong, we can't both be caught," said Cathal, reassuring him.

Cathal crawled down the side of the hill leading to the bunker entrance. He crept up to the entrance cautiously, only to find the large metal door propped slightly open.

He became much more nervous at this. Things weren't going their way right now; Gabriel wasn't around, the entrance was unguarded, and the door was propped open. It was almost as if the Germans were welcoming them to come in and take the stone.

"Come on," Cathal said to himself, trying to piece together the motivation for going through the propped door. What dangers were hidden inside, waiting for him? He only needed the image of Keela to pop up in his head to remind him of why he was here—to save Keela and the world.

Cathal took a deep breath and pushed the door open a little further in to fit his head so that he could peer inside. The lights were on, but yet again, there were no guards, only an empty metal stairwell descending several floors down.

He squeezed his entire body through the opening as silently as possible and started to tiptoe down the metal steps to make as little noise as possible. The concrete walls were lined with cracks from the shakes of bombings. On he went, ever so clandestine, step by step, down to the bottom of the long stairwell.

Clank! Cathal whipped around to see Liam at the top; the door slammed shut. The sound echoed through the stairwell and down into the unknown hallway. If looks could strike down another human, Liam would have been on the floor knocked out.

Cathal's eyes stared down Liam as he tiptoed toward him. "Sorry!" Liam whispered, looking embarrassed.

"I told you to wait!" whispered Cathal in the softest tone.

"I'm sorry, but you may need my help."

"If they didn't know we were here, they do now." Cathal turned around and continued his way down the steps with Liam following close.

They finally reached the bottom of the steps, which led to a dimly lit hallway. They had two options, two passages; they could go either to the right or to the left.

Cathal, looking down the left, tilted his head slightly around the corner and whipped his head back. "A gun turret. This isn't good."

"What is a gun turret?"

Cathal explained, "Basically, it's a powerful gun that will annihilate us if we get in its way. The barrel is sticking out of the wall. There is usually a man on the other side of that wall, ready to shoot at whatever is in front of him. He has complete protection."

"So what are we supposed to do? We can't defend ourselves."

"Well, there's nothing else we can do but go for it. We've come this far. We just have to hope that no one is behind that gun."

Cathal looked down the right side of the hallway and quickly pulled his head back. "The left side has the gun and a dead end. The right side leads to an end with an opening to the left. We go right."

"How do we know if someone is behind that gun?"

"We don't."

Liam gulped in anxiety. "So how are we going to do this?"

Cathal stepped out into the hallway. Liam reached for him to pull him back, but it was too late. He stared down the barrel of the gun. Nothing. He began to walk closer toward it. Still nothing. Cathal turned around and made his way back to Liam.

"I don't think there is anyone behind it. If there was, I'd be dead by now. We are going to walk down the right hallway. I will be facing the direction we are headed in. Liam, your back will be toward me. You'll be facing the gun."

Liam tried to chime in, but Cathal continued. "If you hear anything, anything at all, you drop down to the floor. I will do the same. We might have a chance at dodging the initial round of gunfire."

"And what would we do after that? Run?"

"Precisely. Let's go now. We've already wasted too much time." Cathal moved into the hallway, and Liam followed, positioning himself back to back with Cathal.

They slowly moved down the hallway. Liam tried to listen for anything involving the gun that stared back at him, but the pounding of his heart took all his attention. Step by step, they got closer until they reached the end and stopped. Cathal peered around the corner.

"Another gun, not too far though. Let's continue."

This time, Cathal faced the barrel as he walked toward it. Liam followed, walking backward.

The stench of human waste began to seep into their noses. Liam gagged. They rounded another corner. In front of them was another hallway, and to the right of it was a wooden door. Cathal grabbed the knob and turned it, pushing the door open.

A small room lay before them. The room was large enough to fit one man, a chair, and part of the gun turret to fire. The room was empty. Still not one guard was present. Cathal picked up a Karabiner 98k rifle, which was leaned up against the back wall, and a knife resting on the chair. He came out of the room and handed the knife to Liam.

"That's it?" Liam appeared upset about what he had gotten.

"That's it. We aren't prepared if we are ambushed. These were the only two weapons available."

They continued to walk down the hallway and found another door on the right. The smell of feces and urine was now unbearable. Cathal opened the door to a dark room with holes in the ground and said, "A bathroom. Moving on."

The ceiling crept down lower as they moved further down the hall. Now crouching, they moved forward. The walls were covered in various paintings of war— SS soldiers standing tall and proud. Some were holding shields and pointing them at civilians.

At the end of the hallway, in front of another wooden door, Cathal reached for the knob, turned it, and pushed it open. A small dark room was before them. There was a table in the middle with chairs around it, and a map covered the top of the table with markings in various positions.

"Must be strategic military positions," Cathal mentioned.

"Behind the table, there's a chest," Liam pointed, grabbing Cathal's attention.

Cathal rushed for the chest and opened it. It was empty.

The lights flashed on, blinding Liam and Cathal momentarily. When their vision came to, the room wasn't as empty as it had been when they had first entered. Four SS soldiers stood there with their rifles pointed right at both of them.

A laugh was heard from behind. Skorn pushed through the middle of the soldiers. Cathal wanted to knock the smirk right off him.

"Nice outfits." Skorn smiled, looking at their robes. "Is this what you were looking for?" Skorn smirked as he tossed up and down a shiny obsidian stone in his palm.

"Sky or Wind, I believe? Do you really believe that these stones together hold the power to stop us? Even with all the stones, the Elluna are no match for the Tarnok. They've been planning their arrival forever. It is our time to rule."

"How'd you know where it was supposed to be?" Cathal's tone became even more angry.

Skorn smiled, now gazing into the stone. "I can't believe you think that low of me. I'm insulted. I know much more than you think. I have not only this one but also Viktor's stone, so you don't have to bother looking for that one. And if you haven't noticed, I've made some friends along the way."

He pointed at the soldiers with him, their guns still pointed at Liam and Cathal.

Cathal whipped out his rifle in one last attempt to save him and his cousin. *Click, click.* The rifle failed to fire off any rounds.

Skorn shook his head. "I planted that rifle."

Liam quickly threw his knife at a soldier next to Skorn, but Skorn quickly caught the knife in midair.

"Should have picked the knife, Cathal," said Skorn. "I think you would have had a better chance than he did." Skorn nodded to a soldier who walked over to Liam, striking him in the head with the butt of his rifle, knocking him to the ground unconscious.

"So, I guess, this is it?" Cathal questioned Skorn as he placed the rifle down on the floor. How could he have been that stupid and unprepared for this bunker? Door wide open, no guards, and a light rifle. He really got outmatched this time.

Skorn put on his evil smirk that Cathal hated so much. "No, no, no, Cathal. Your journey is over, but your life…Well, you're going to wish it was over. I'm not going to kill you just yet."

Skorn made his way toward Cathal. "I'm going to make you watch as I torture and kill your cousin. Then I'm going to kill you, and then I'm going to go and have my way with Keela!"

Skorn had already burned her alive, but he felt it would torture him more—the thought of what he was going to possibly do to her after Cathal was gone.

Cathal went to swing at Skorn, but he was too late. Skorn tornado-kicked Cathal right in the head, knocking him to the ground unconscious.

CHAPTER TWENTY-TWO

S korn lifted a pail of water off the ground, walked over to a large pillar, and hurled the water on to Liam and Cathal, who were tied up and passed out against it. Cathal and Liam immediately came to. Startled, they tried to break free but to no avail: the ropes that bound them to the pillar were securely tied.

"Feeling a little hazy?" Skorn laughed.

"What did you do to us?" Cathal, a little groggy, took some time to respond.

"You've been drugged. A high dosage, I might add. You've been out for several days."

"Where are we?" Cathal asked, thinking he might actually get an answer from Skorn. He thought the chances of escape seemed very slim at this point.

"Doesn't matter where you are. What matters is that you have failed. It's over." Confidence oozed from Skorn's face.

Cathal tried to focus and use his bracelet to get out of the current situation, but it was of no use. Whatever Skorn had been administering to him was surely working.

"You've been drugged, Cathal. You can't focus clearly enough to do anything. It should almost be time for another dose. Don't worry, we plan on keeping you that way until we finish what we are doing." Skorn paused for a moment and began to smirk. "And then we will kill you."

Skorn continued to taunt Cathal, but Cathal stopped focusing on his voice and started to focus on his surroundings. If he couldn't use his traveling power, he was going to have to use his training to escape. He looked around the wrecked, war-torn building, which appeared to have been a church before the war. The walls and ceilings weren't intact; there were huge holes in the walls and in the roof, probably from explosions. Several pews were still where they should have been, while others were knocked down, missing, or destroyed into fragments of what they used to be. Cathal calculated about ten soldiers patrolling the church grounds on the inside. He had no clue as to how many could possibly be patrolling outside.

Skorn continued, "I have moved your precious stones here. It was quite easy. I now have the Sky Stone and Viktor's centerpiece."

"Easier for me to get both. You did my job. I thank you," Cathal replied, trying to regain the upper hand.

"I brought them here because if you happened to notice, you are surrounded by one of the largest and most powerful armies the world has ever seen. Not to mention that you are currently powerless and that they are currently under my command. So if you, by any chance, were able to get by me, well…that's not happening."

"I still have more stones than you do, and I will be able to unlock their powers." Cathal knew this wasn't true, but he needed to play at Skorn's game.

Skorn laughed and strolled around the two of them, both tied helplessly. "You can't trick me. You need all five of the stones together to unlock their power. So long as I have just one stone, it's over. You've failed."

Skorn continued to rant, staring into a half-shattered stained-glass window of what used to be some sort of religious icon. "Terranos and the rest of the Tarnok will come, and they will rule this world with me and the rest of the Tarnen at their side. I will be bathed in glory! Rewarded greatly for my deeds! I will make sure you are there to witness everything!"

A door in the back of the church behind the remains of an altar slammed open, interrupting Skorn. Three Nazi soldiers appeared and walked toward them, one of whom looked to be of high rank. The other two appeared to be his personal guards.

Skorn met them halfway. They conversed, whispering in German and looking back at Cathal and Liam sporadically.

Liam started to squirm around, attempting to make some progress toward an escape. "What's the plan?" he whispered.

"I'm not sure," Cathal responded; he continued to look around for some possible escape.

Skorn shouted from where he met the three soldiers. "My friends, it's been a pleasure. I have some matters to attend to. I will be back. Don't worry, I'm leaving you in great hands!"

The soldiers stepped toward them as Skorn left through the same door, the one behind the broken-down altar.

"Good morning, gentleman. My name is Colonel Bach, and these two are my personal guards."

Liam and Cathal stared blankly in front of themselves, completely ignoring their presence.

"I want to ask you some questions, and I highly recommend you answer them in the utmost sincerity," Bach continued.

The two remained unresponsive to his words.

"We can do it that way if you'd like." Bach nodded to his two soldiers, who walked over to each of them and started to assault them.

Cathal didn't crack. Swing by swing, blow by blow, he remained motionless. Blood dripped from his blank face. Liam took it a little differently: he was not nearly ready for the pain he was about to endure. With each blow, he screamed in agony. The soldier attacking him loved it. He fed off Liam's screams, and the more he screamed, the more he attacked him.

Cathal's soldier wasn't happy with his results and took the butt end of his rifle to his face. Blood splattered along the stone wall next to them as he slipped to the floor.

"Stop!" Bach said as he noticed that Cathal's sleeve was pushed up as he slipped to the ground. A gold reflection seeped into his eyes. "Could it be the bracelet? This is what allows you to travel through time? Does it not?"

Cathal could barely open his eyes from the beating he had just took. All he saw was red; all he tasted was blood. Still, he remained silent.

"Let's take a look at this." The colonel bent down and slid the bracelet right off his hand. Cathal didn't flinch.

"I'll be right back." Colonel Bach gazed down in awe at the bracelet in hand. "If they move, shoot them." Bach exited through the door behind the altar with the bracelet in hand.

CHAPTER TWENTY-THREE

New York City, USA—January 22, 1999

Troy took a large puff from his cigar and placed it down on the ashtray. Skorn entered his office with a confident swagger.

"You wanted to see me, boss?" asked Skorn.

"Boss?" That word enraged Troy. "You're supposed to do what the boss says! And what did you do?" Troy's fists slammed into his desk. "You went back and slaughtered that whole village!"

Troy screamed at Skorn, who was taken aback with surprise.

Confused, Skorn answered, "I took some matters into my own hands, but the results speak for themselves. We are in much better position now than we were before."

Troy grabbed the cigar and placed it back in his mouth to get some more puffs. "Why would you do such a thing?" he asked.

Then he got up from his desk chair and made his way toward the front of his desk and said, "That action could have screwed up history as we know it."

"Did it?" Skorn replied with a snobby tone.

Troy sat on the front edge of his desk, more relaxed. "Right now, no, but who knows when he finds out what will happen?"

He took another puff, trying to enjoy something in his life at that moment. "So explain what happened at the village. Why was it such a success to you?" he asked.

"I didn't do it all on my own. A group of Vikings raiding the countryside were camped not far away. I promised them riches for a simple request—to take Keela for my own."

"Did Cathal come?"

"No, unfortunately not. I waited for him. I tied Keela up. She called out his name, but he never came."

"Did you kill her?" Troy's relaxed mood began to become tense again.

"I did. I set her ablaze as I left. I did meet someone else," Skorn began to add, trying to change Troy's attention. "I believe it was the man who had bestowed Cathal with his quest. He mentioned the Tarnok just before I ended his life."

"What was his name?" Troy crushed the remaining cigar in his hand and threw the remains into the garbage alongside his desk.

"An old man. He put up quite a fight."

"What was his name?" Troy interrupted him. His patience was wearing thin.

"Crowley."

Troy stood up, and his face became a ghostly white. Skorn had never seen it so pale, as Troy became suddenly enraged after hearing Crowley's name.

"You are an imbecile!" Troy yelled, whipping around and throwing everything off his desk in rage. "This will be the demise of you! Of us!"

Skorn moved back several steps. "I'm doing my job! You wanted me to take care of Cathal. This is my way of doing it. I've slaughtered anyone close to him. And we currently have two stones. In addition, we have captured Cathal and his cousin. It's over, Troy! You should be thanking me. We've won! A victory for all because of me."

Skorn's words only added gasoline to the fire of Troy's anger, who was now behind his desk, staring out into the city skyline. "You're a fool! Once he finds out about what you've done, he will come at you with everything he's got!"

Skorn stepped toward Troy, not happy about his own boss's reaction. "No, he will be dead or broken!"

"He will have nothing to live for but ending you. It's my fault—you weren't ready. I trusted you with a job you couldn't handle."

A bored look rushed over Skorn's face. "I think you need to step down and get out of my way."

"Know your place, boy!" Troy turned around and jumped over his desk, kicking Skorn in midair and sending him back clear through the wall and into the hallway.

Smoke covered the new hole in the wall, leaving Skorn's whereabouts a mystery. Troy tried to see through the smoke, but it was too late. Two knives flew through the smoke and landed tightly in Troy's chest.

Troy was completely shocked at what this conversation had turned into. He looked down at the two blades, practically hidden in his chest. His clothes were dripping with blood. He heard steps rushing toward him. Skorn appeared through the smoke, running straight for him. He jumped at Troy, knocking him backward into the desk, and then landed on top of his chest.

Skorn crouched over him, like a gargoyle statue resting on top of an old Gothic-style building, and said, "People should know when they don't have it anymore."

Troy stared into Skorn's eyes, still in complete shock at what had just unfolded.

Skorn reached down and pulled out one of the knives; blood spilled out of the wound. "I think, for the arrival, they'll be greeted by a new leader of the Tarnen. Someone who gets things done," Skorn said.

Skorn positioned the blade over Troy's neck, who still was speechless and stared back at him, and said, "Good-bye."

He lifted the blade one more time and swung right through his throat, ending his former master's life. Blood spread across his desk, including the pages of an old ancient-looking book that caught Skorn's eye.

He hopped off the desk and walked around to look over the book. Brushing the blood away from a particular entry, he said to himself, "This must have been a diary of some sort for Troy."

Maius 333

Constantinopolis

I've been swayed to join forces with the Tarnen. They have given me one month's time to get out and enter their ranks. This was a decision that took much thought, for I love my brothers and sisters in Elluna's Guard, more specifically my dear friend Crowley. Unfortunately, I don't believe in their ideals anymore. I tried to convince Crowley to come with me, but he thought that it was absurd and that I was only joking.

"I had no idea Crowley meant anything to you." Skorn looked over at Troy's lifeless body. He continued to read on.

Iunius 333
Constantinopolis
Crowley has been going frantic as of late with these visions of the future. He's been scribing down specific dates, which he called the utmost importance to on a scroll. I must stay until he has completed this. I believe him, and before I leave, I must have the knowledge of these dates. This most certainly will win me favor within the Tarnen. Once he is finished, I will do the unimaginable and join with the Tarnen. Oh, please brother Crowley, join me.

Keep me strong, Terranos, Lord and Ruler of all.

Things started to make a lot more sense to Skorn. He knew Troy's power was to never age, but he didn't think he had been around this long. This was also the reason he went ballistic after hearing about the death of his once-close friend. Skorn flipped much farther into the book, which seemed to go on forever.

October 12, 1992
New York City
Skorn's training has gone extremely well. He's the best student I've ever had. I must admit, at first I took him in to make him an elite soldier and follower of the Tarnen only. He has turned

into so much more than that. He's family. I love him now, like the son I never had. I am so proud of him and will continue to be there to support him always.

Skorn closed the book. A tear fell from his eye and mixed into the blood of his former master and father.

CHAPTER TWENTY-FOUR

The run-down church had nothing to offer Cathal as he continued to attempt to piece together any possible escape in his head.

"There's no escape," the guard told him, laughing at him. "Maybe you would see a little better if you wiped that blood out of your eyes."

Cathal forced a smirk.

Liam continued to wince in pain from the beating he had just taken. Still, he attempted to break free from the ropes holding him down. The guard trained in on him, laughing at his meager efforts.

"I do feel a lot better already," Cathal thought as he started to fake the pain to make the guards believe he was in the same shape as Liam. "Almost at full strength." Whatever drug they had been injecting him with had almost run its course.

Other guards continued to make their regular patrolling routes inside the church. Cathal thought, "This church must be a lot more important than it looks to have this many guards."

The door behind the altar opened, and everyone turned their heads in its direction. Colonel Bach stood in the doorway, discussing something with someone unseen in the room. Cathal looked right past him and saw a table. "It could have a map with specific military positions. I could use this to my benefit," he thought.

Colonel Bach closed the door and walked back toward them with an irritated look over his face. "It's a fake. Cathal, you've wasted my time."

"No, it's not fake, Colonel. Rest assured it is very real. The only problem is that you are not me." Cathal smiled finally, getting the upper hand.

Bach's face became more agitated as Cathal continued, "How do you think we got here?"

"Doesn't matter!" Bach snapped back. "Kill them both!"

The guards raised their rifles at their intended victims.

"Wait! I can help you!" Cathal shouted in desperation.

"How could you possibly help me? You and your partner are helpless. You are done." Bach gave his men the go-ahead signal for the kill.

"No! Don't you want to move up in the ranks of the Third Reich? I can help you rise to the top!"

"You're just stalling for time, Cathal. I have extremely important matters to attend to. I must be going." Bach turned around and started to walk away. The guards aligned their eyesight with the scope.

"I can get you on board a US battleship! You can commandeer it in the blink of an eye!" He used one last attempt to save them.

Bach paused in his motion and turned around. "You have my attention. Go on."

Bach strode back toward him. The curiosity exploded from within.

"What are you doing?" Liam yelled at him.

"Shut up, Liam. I am trying to save our lives."

"Speak, Cathal. You have only moments to persuade me with your proposal. You've wasted too much time as it is." Bach sat down cross-legged in a pew.

"Don't you want to get close to the Führer? I know all the locations of the US naval ships."

"We've spotted them. We know roughly where they are. Our navy is quite powerful. We don't need help there." Bach was shooting his idea down immediately.

Cathal smiled. "Colonel, you don't understand what I am saying. I can get you onboard. I can get you into the control room through teleportation. And from there, you could easily take over the ship."

"That's impressive, but what then? There is an army of soldiers onboard each."

Cathal started to laugh. "I can get you to the bridge. Then we can take it over and fire on other US ships from that location. You could take out a huge chunk of their power."

"But what about getting off? Are you going to leave us there to get captured and become prisoners of war?" Bach tried to find every loophole in his offering, even though it did entice him.

"Aren't you forgetting one small thing? I teleported you onto that ship. I can easily teleport you off that ship. Think about it, Bach. A national hero. Think about what will come when we succeed."

Bach had a smile that extended ear to ear. "I like the sound of that."

"If I do this for you, do I have your word that you'll let Liam and me go?"

"Cut the ropes, and release them," Bach ordered his men, and they knelt down and cut the ropes constricting the two guys, using their knives.

Cathal stood up with ease; he was now fully recovered. He walked over to Liam, who was still struggling, and pulled him up.

"I can't believe you're—" Liam was interrupted with a look Cathal gave him. He knew this was the kind of look that meant that he should shut up and stop talking.

"So, Cathal, what next?" Bach asked.

"I need to see that map you have in the other room. And I am going to need my bracelet back."

"Move." Bach signaled the guards, and they pushed them in the direction of the room with guns pressed to their backs. Bach followed.

"Trust me, everything will be all right," Cathal reassured Liam, who nodded while limping along, like a wounded animal.

The room they arrived in was empty except for four chairs and a table, which had a map of the European Theater of World War II. Plastic markers were positioned all over the map, on the Mediterranean and the Atlantic. Cathal studied the placements and said, "I guess the light markers are your ships and subs, while the dark markers are the enemies?"

Bach nodded. "Where to?"

"What's today's date?" Cathal asked.

"June seventh," Bach answered.

Cathal stared intently at the positions and pointed to a specific area where markers were more abundant. "This is actually pretty accurate for this date," Cathal said.

That information was key for his plan to work. "We shall take a small unit here. There is a destroyer here, the USS *Glennon*," Cathal stated, looking at three markers in the Mediterranean. It was partially accurate, but they didn't need to know that.

He pointed to a marker in the middle of two other markers.

"We are sitting ducks in the middle! That is suicide!" Bach responded with agitation.

"Colonel, if we are in the middle, attack one side. The other side isn't going to know what happened until it's too late. By that point, we would have already started to attack both of them." Cathal completely sold him on that point.

"All right, I like the plan. How do we do this?" Bach asked.

"First, I'm going to need my bracelet back," he insisted, staring at the golden piece as if it were a long-lost friend he hadn't seen in quite some time.

"And then?" Bach still was hesitant to give him back his bracelet.

Cathal smiled. "And then you all grab hold of me—you, your two guards, and Liam. And then I take us to their bridge, and the rest will be history."

"Not so fast. Klaus, come in here, please." Another soldier entered the room. "Klaus, you are going to watch this man and hold him at gunpoint until I get back." Bach pointed at a pale-faced Liam.

Liam stared at Cathal, who winked. "It's OK, Liam. Everything will be fine. We are going to help Colonel Bach with several heroic victories and be back before you know it. And then we'll be free."

Liam nodded his head in pain and winced. He didn't have whatever remarkable healing abilities Cathal somehow managed to have.

Cathal pointed at his bracelet in Bach's hands. "I'm going to need that now," Cathal said.

Bach made his way over to him and grabbed his arm. "Klaus, you watch him. If he moves, kill him. Leon, Bruno, grab his shoulders. I don't want him doing anything quickly before I put this on him."

"Ain't I going to get a gun?" Cathal asked.

Bach laughed as he gripped Cathal's arm in one hand and slid the bracelet on with the other.

Cathal immediately felt relieved. His powers seemed to be flowing through him once more. Cathal looked over at Bach and asked, "Are you ready?" Bach nodded in agreement. Cathal smiled at Liam, reassuring him that everything would be all right. A blue light flashed, and the room became empty except for Klaus and Liam.

"I know, guys. I really miss her." John threw down his cigarette and stomped it out. The other seven US soldiers huddled in a circle on the deck, finishing up their cigs. The men of the USS *Glennon* were taking a quick smoke break outside on the deck of this magnificent war machine before they had to return to their posts.

A flashing light formed in the middle of the men. Startled, they jumped back. Eight handguns immediately were out and trained on the light, which started to fade. In its place were four humans.

"Don't move, and drop your weapons!" John ordered the four men.

Bach looked furious as Leon and Bruno slowly placed their guns to the floor. Cathal smiled at Bach, who stared back at him stonily.

"You're coming with us," John ordered.

CHAPTER TWENTY-FIVE

Cathal, Leon, Bruno, and Bach walked single file down the cramped hallway of the destroyer with guns aimed directly on them; they were defeated. Leon was first followed by Bruno, Bach, and then Cathal. Bach twisted his head around to stare at Cathal.

"Turn around!" a guard shouted. Bach looked forward.

They walked hunched over down the cramped hallways, turning in several directions. Cathal wanted to teleport right that very moment, but he couldn't risk it. Crowley specifically said not to use teleportation powers in front of anyone else, for people not privy to the situation might witness it, and this could change the course of history. He messed that one up by teleporting in the middle of them already, Cathal thought. But he specifically chose this destroyer because he knew it would be sunk in three days, losing twenty-five men. He was taking a risk hoping the men on the smoke break would all be men who died onboard.

John held onto Cathal's shoulder tightly as they continued through the labyrinth of the USS *Glennon*. Another reason he couldn't teleport was that he didn't want to take him as well. John's grip clamped down and restrained Cathal to a sudden stop.

"You guys take those Kraut fools to the holding cell," John ordered and looked at Cathal. "I'm going to take this other suspicious character in robes to the conference room. Here, go in there."

Bach whipped his head around and spat in Cathal's direction, but it missed him and landed on John's face. A guard pushed Bach forward as they disappeared around the corner. John looked as if he had been violated.

Cathal opened the small door and pushed in. The room was very tiny, similar to an interrogation room. There was a small metal table and two chairs but not much room for anything else.

"Here, sit," said John. "I'll be right back." John pointed to the chair at the far end and spoke very slowly as if he thought Cathal wouldn't be able to understand too clearly. Cathal smirked and nodded. John stared at him as Cathal walked over to the chair to sit. "Good. One minute. I need to clean up." John spoke even slower this time and closed the door.

"Finally, a moment alone," Cathal thought. Then he closed his eyes, concentrated, and then vanished within a second.

A minute later, the door opened with John holding a cup of coffee. He dropped the cup, which shattered into pieces on the floor. "This is not good," he said.

CHAPTER TWENTY-SIX

A flash of blue light appeared in the map room. Cathal appeared as it dissipated. There was not a single sound from the teleportation, and Cathal reflected on how good he had become at it.

He looked around the room; there was no sign of Liam or the guard, Klaus; there was just the table with the map. He looked down and smiled at the small marker on the map, indicating the ship he had just left Bach and his men on.

Cathal heard voices coming from the room adjacent to him. He crept over to the entryway into that room and peered around the corner. Liam was on his knees, and Klaus stood above him with his handgun pressed to the back of Liam's head.

Cathal quietly made his way behind Klaus, wrapped his arms around his neck, and pulled him to the floor.

Klaus only had a moment to panic before he was reduced to an unconscious state. He quickly grabbed the gun and stood back over Liam, who had not moved or noticed what had just occurred.

"You can get up now," Cathal ordered Liam.

Liam slowly opened his eyes and turned to see that it was not his captor standing over him but his cousin. Energy returned to his battered face. "What happened to Colonel Bach?"

Cathal smiled and said, "Let's just say he will be moving up in the ranks of his enemies' prisoner status and not of the Third Reich's status."

"Nice move, but what if he tells them about your teleportation?" Liam questioned Cathal's decision.

"The ship I teleported to sinks in three days, unfortunately. Many people die—it's disheartening to say, but I was taking a risk on who would have actually witnessed this and have time to tell others about it. It was all I could think of." Cathal justified his decision.

"Terrible, these wars are," Liam sighed.

Cathal leaned over Klaus and smacked him in his face. Klaus came to and quickly went to defend himself, but Cathal swiftly pressed his boot to Klaus's neck and forced a gun barrel to his forehead immediately to end his retaliation.

"I need to know where Skorn has placed the stones," said Cathal.

"I will never tell you!" Klaus was saying what he could with the boot to his neck.

"I wish you didn't make me do this." Cathal tucked the gun into the backside of his pants.

"What are you doing?" Liam questioned Cathal's action.

"Relax." Cathal looked down at Klaus and then placed his index finger over several spots of Klaus's body in a specific order.

Klaus instantaneously began to shriek in agony. "Make it stop! Make it stop! I'll tell you!"

Cathal performed another motion of pressure points, relieving the pain. "As you were saying?"

"Skorn has sent the stones to be placed on a train." Klaus was still catching his breath.

"Where is this train?" Cathal pressed down more on his neck.

"There is a train yard about twenty kilometers north of here."

"When is it set to leave?"

Klaus took in some more air. "It is set to leave in about one hour. Now please let me go."

"No problem. You've been very helpful." Cathal tapped him in several spots, and Klaus went right to sleep.

Liam smiled and said, "You're going to have to teach me that one day, among other things."

"After we save the world, I'm sure I'll have some time, but we need to find, and get aboard, this train as soon as possible." Cathal took out the gun. "Let's go."

They exited out of the broken-down church and stepped out onto the desolate city streets. The roads before them were completely destroyed and filled with debris. Cars and trucks with smashed windows were either flipped over or on their side. As they walked the streets, they rummaged through each one of the vehicles they came in contact with to see if it would fit their travel needs, but each one was completely inoperable.

Buildings were half standing, and there were big gaping holes in many of them—the results of heavy artillery fire. In many buildings, they could see right into the second and third floors. Some were office buildings; some were once living rooms and kitchens.

Liam and Cathal eventually stumbled upon a bridge at the outskirts of the city, but there was still no sign of transportation. The bridge had holes large enough that one could drive his or her car over the road and easily fall into the flowing river below.

Liam stopped; his eyes fixed on something in the distance. "Cathal, stop," he whispered.

Cathal stopped, turned around, and waited for Liam to continue.

Liam pointed straight ahead. "Look, does that smoke look natural?"

A little ways after the bridge, smoke puffed out of the corner of a building at about the height of a man's head.

"I'm impressed. That looks like cigarette smoke. It might be a soldier." Cathal nodded and, feeling impressed, added, "Nice eyes, Liam."

Liam smiled.

"You need to wait here. I'll go up ahead," Cathal ordered Liam.

"What? I spotted it. I should be coming with you," Liam answered discouragingly.

"Look," Cathal said and paused, looking at his gun, "we only have one weapon. The less people, the less chance of being caught. Let me see what's up ahead, and then I'll come back to you."

Liam agreed. "You're right. Hurry back."

He crouched down next to a broken-down car, which was hanging partially off the edge of the bridge.

Cathal stepped lightly across the bridge toward the smoke, which had now disappeared. He kept his eyes fixated on the corner of that building, knowing that someone could have just been there.

As he made his way closer to the building, he noticed pieces of gravel on the ground, bouncing around ever so slightly. The closer he got, the more these granules seemed to move.

He made it to the corner and pressed his back up against the brick wall. His back vibrated as it tried to stay hugged to the wall. He took a breath and peered around the corner. A soldier, his back facing him, was walking in the opposite direction. But what the man was walking toward made his heart sink into his stomach.

Four other soldiers were heading toward his direction, surrounding a Panzer IV German war tank. The ground started to shake even more.

Cathal whipped his head back out of view. His heart started to race uncontrollably; it felt like it was going to rip out of his chest. He had read about the Panzer IV, that it was literally an unstoppable piece of war machinery. Several Allied tanks barely stood a chance against them. What could he possibly do with a handgun and a defenseless Liam against five German soldiers and a Panzer IV tank?

The ground began to shake even more; they were getting closer. He peered once more around the corner. In the distance, a soldier had spotted Cathal's head poking out. He started to scream and point in his direction. The other soldiers, now aware of his position, started to run and fire in his direction.

Bullets hit the bricks, just inches from his head, sending red shards in all directions. He peered around once more; the Panzer's main gun was now turned toward the corner he was hiding behind.

Cathal jumped from the wall and started to sprint toward the bridge as he heard the main gunfire. The blast hit the corner of the building, sending the entire wall, where he had just been standing, in all directions. Bricks went flying everywhere. Cathal flew through the air about thirty feet and finally slammed into the ground.

Liam screamed in horror as he ran to Cathal and helped him up.

"They have a tank!" Cathal screamed.

They sprinted across the bridge, jumping over random holes, and quickly hid behind the first building they reached.

"How many?" Liam asked, still trying to catch his breath.

"There were five soldiers on the ground, and there must be at least three inside the Panzer."

Liam looked through the crumbling wall of the building they were hiding behind. They saw five men, alert and with guns out, surrounding a large tank; the men were hustling across the bridge.

Cathal looked down at the Browning Hi-Power pistol he took off Klaus and said, "One gun, nine rounds. Eight men and a tank."

Liam giggled and said, "That seems fair." Cathal joined in the laughter.

"Listen, they don't know about you," said Cathal. He paused a brief moment to look through the crack. They were getting closer. "I'm going to keep their attention, take some of them out while I can. You're going to need to go around behind them and get a weapon off each soldier. I'll try to kill some, and you grab a weapon off their dead bodies."

Liam nodded and said, "OK." He looked through the hole once again. He only saw two soldiers and the back of the tank. "They're close. What in God Almighty is a tank? That is frightening!"

"All right, Liam. This is it." Cathal reached out his hand to Liam, who shook it in turn. "Go now, and wait for me to act. I'll try to drop some of them soon."

Liam gave him one last look, turned, and ran off around the corner of the building and out of sight.

Cathal felt the vibrations of the tank more than ever before. Even his own footing started to shake beneath him. The five soldiers were very close. He heard the soldiers speaking in German. Even over the tank's rumblings, he was able to comprehend what they said, and they were saying that they thought Cathal was by himself.

He took a deep breath and looked to his left again. Liam was gone. He readied his pistol and stood up.

Running across the street, Cathal ran out in front of the soldiers and fired. Everything slowed down in his mind as this happened: his movements and the soldiers' reactions all seemed to take forever, but he knew this all happened more quickly in the eyes of the enemy troops.

The first round hit a still unsuspecting soldier right in the head. He fired a second at another soldier, just grazing his shoulder. Then he fired a third round at the same soldier still running in full stride across the road and made another head shot.

He now ran to hide from the three remaining soldiers and the tank, which began firing once again at his location. Cathal slid behind a broken-down jeep and said to himself, "Six bullets, six men, and one tank."

He twisted his head around the jeep. The three soldiers and the tank cautiously moved in his direction, guns cocked and ready to fire. One soldier yelled at the tank, pointing at the vehicle, "Time to move!"

Cathal hopped up and dashed away as the main gun of the tank fired another round at the jeep, sending it high in the sky and exploding into flames. He turned and fired two more shots at another soldier. One more down.

Bullets flew right past his body as he sprinted his way into another crumbling building. The smoke from the explosion of the jeep filled the nearby street, momentarily halting the Nazis' assault on Cathal. "C'mon, Liam…," Cathal whispered to himself. Four bullets, five men, and one tank, he reminded himself.

The wind blew the smoke away. He could now see the two remaining soldiers on foot, arguing over where he probably was hiding. There was a sound coming from the tank; the hatch popped open, and the tank commander popped his upper body out of the hole. He began yelling and pointing at the building that Cathal was hiding in.

The tank's main gun rotated toward his building to fire. Cathal ran out again and cut across the street as the blast sent more debris in every direction. Cathal turned and took another shot at one of the soldiers, who was already firing in his direction. He hit the soldier right in the head; the man went to the ground.

Cathal continued to dash down the street away from the tank; he looked back but couldn't find the remaining soldier.

A sharp pain shot up his hand and through his arm. His hand that was holding the pistol suddenly went numb and felt lighter; the pistol was gone, shot right out of his clutches. Cathal rounded the corner of another building. No gun, one tank, and four men left. He started to panic.

Cathal moved further down the edge of the building, away from the road. He could feel the ground shake again; they were getting close. He had nothing to defend himself with. "Where are you, Liam?" Cathal thought.

He heard several shots fired. There was the sound of the hatch of the tank opening, some German men screaming, and then a small explosion. Cathal was very confused at what had just taken place.

And then there was silence, absolute silence. Cathal moved ever so cautiously closer to the road; he dragged his body up against the building's brick wall. He slowly looked around the corner to see what had just taken place.

Liam stood smiling, holding two MG 42 machine guns. Behind him, smoke flowed out of the tank's hatch, and the other soldier lay on the ground. "You're welcome!" Liam shouted as he tossed one of the guns into Cathal's hands. Cathal stared at him in shock, but shortly after, he started to chuckle.

"Sorry, it took me a while."

"Not a problem at all," Cathal said, smiling. "Thank you, but we have a train to catch."

"Yes, we do," Liam replied.

CHAPTER TWENTY-SEVEN

They hurried through the streets, retracing their steps, while they glanced at the destruction that had just occurred from their recent altercation. The destruction caused by the tank was clearly evident from the buildings that had previously stood but were now nothing except rubble and smoke.

"Do you think we shall catch that train?"

"We had better catch it," Cathal replied.

"Why? Can't we just teleport to the next open location?" Liam squeezed out the statement while gasping for breath. Cathal was calm and collected while running; it didn't faze him as much as Liam, who wasn't nearly as in shape as him.

"The scroll had specific dates. Skorn changed things when he went to those time periods and took the stones for himself," Cathal explained.

"Then we find Skorn!" Liam replied.

The sun started to disappear between the crumbling buildings as they crossed over the broken-down bridge they had passed over before.

"Liam, if we don't catch this train, it's over. There's no doubt about it." Cathal quickened his pace as the words came out of his mouth.

Liam sprinted to catch up to Cathal. He looked to his right and saw the very corner where he had spotted the cigarette smoke earlier.

Cathal continued, "Skorn changed things. He took the two remaining stones and moved them. The scroll doesn't matter anymore. If we don't catch this train, the stones could be lost forever. We will have nothing else to go on. We can't just teleport out of here and move to the next place. We have no idea where to go."

"I still think we can get Skorn and get him to lead us to them if this fails," Liam replied.

"If we ever see him again. Skorn isn't the type of person who will give up that information."

Liam and Cathal slowed their pace to a stop as they reached the edge of town.

Cathal looked to the right and left. His eyes fixated on something to his left as he ran over to a tarp and pulled it off, revealing just what they needed—a motorcycle with a sidecar.

"This is our best bet to get there on time," Cathal said, staring down at the bike and smiling.

Cathal hopped on the main bike and started the engine. "Get in!"

"I have to get in that little thing?" Liam felt embarrassed.

"Do it now, or I will leave you." Cathal pointed up at a sign several feet away that said "Bahnhof 30 kilometer nördlich." He said, "Klaus lied. The station is thirty kilometers north of here. We can still make it. Get on!"

Liam jumped in the sidecar, and before he could say anything, Cathal slammed on the accelerator and went barreling down the road.

They sped down the half-gravel half-dirt road, with fields surrounding them on all sides. Smoke in the distance arose around them on both sides, indicating the presence nearby of many destroyed military vehicles. "One of the costs of war," Cathal explained.

"This time period is awful," Liam stated as he thought back to the destruction he saw in the city as well as in China during this same time period.

"Every generation experiences terrible tragedy. History often does seem to repeat itself over and over." Cathal swerved over a random spot in the road.

"What was that? I almost fell out!" screamed Liam.

"Land mine. There are plenty of them out here."

Liam looked back at the torn-up road and saw nothing indicating a land mine. "Your vision must be out of this world because I didn't see anything on the ground back there showing signs of whatever this land mine is."

Cathal swerved again. "Another one. I read about what they looked like, and I saw pictures, and I guess I've got a heightened sense right now. A land mine is kind of like a weapon that explodes when you hit it. We don't want that."

Cathal's eyes fixated on the road. Time was running out. The sun had descended, resting just above the tree line, to the right past the fields. There were no more fields to the left of them—only woods. The road was tightly bordering a thick forest.

For several moments, silence kicked in between the two of them. It was a brief moment of rest from the action they had been getting used to. Cathal glanced over to Liam, who had been staring at Cathal driving the bike.

"This is amazing. So much different than horses," Liam stated.

Cathal laughed and said, "I'd stop and let you drive to practice, but we don't really have that time. I'll just show you, and hopefully, you can pick it up quickly."

While continuing to drive, Cathal showed Liam how to accelerate, brake, and maneuver the bike. Cathal remembered that when he was younger, on the rare occasions when he did hang out with Liam, that Liam's mind was like a sponge and would absorb everything rather quickly.

"Wow, that's it? I've got to get a chance to do this." Liam smiled.

"That's it." Cathal smiled.

"So, Cathal, after all this is done, you will try to start a family with Keela?" Liam changed the subject.

He smiled. "After all this is done. She's why I'm doing it. End this threat, and I can be with her in peace."

"Aye, you snagged an amazing lady there." Liam smiled with a sigh.

"Something wrong, Liam? You have your sights on any girl?"

"No, cousin. I wish, but hopefully, someday someone like Keela will come into my life. Right now, my concern is making sure you have a future with her so that one day I might have my own Keela. I hope I am worthy enough to aid you on this quest and that I'm not slowing you down."

Cathal said, "Well, I just was involved with a situation with that tank, where it was pretty much the end of me. You definitely proved your worth there. And you've proved it elsewhere."

"Thanks, it really means—" Liam started with a smile but was interrupted by bullets flying right past both of their heads.

Liam turned his head around and saw a man on another bike, firing right at them. Two other Nazi cargo trucks were following the man.

The distance between them and the man firing upon them closed. He was on a single motorcycle with no attachment like Liam and Cathal.

Cathal did the best he could, trying to speed up, but having the weight of two people instead of one wasn't any help. Soon, they were able to make out his face through the Nazi uniform he had on; it was Skorn.

Liam quickly readied his gun.

"Fire, Liam!" Cathal shouted to Liam as he began to weave among the broken-down vehicles on the road.

Liam fired several rounds at Skorn, which all missed, as he maneuvered his way around the road. Skorn fired back and then screamed something at the two cargo trucks beside him.

The back tarps on the cargo trucks flew off, unveiling about a dozen men inside who were all armed with machine guns.

Liam's eyes widened, looking back at Skorn, who was now surrounded by almost thirty men, armed and staring them down.

"You can't win, Cathal!" Skorn screamed.

"You might want to just glance back!" Liam shouted at Cathal.

Cathal took a quick glance back and whipped his head back around to face the obstacles ahead of him and Liam. He took a quick gulp; the problems never end. "Stall him! Give me some time to get closer to the station!" Cathal shouted to Liam.

As if it wasn't enough trouble to avoid broken-down vehicles, Cathal now had to swerve between live civilian automobiles.

"You have the stones! What more do you want from us?" Liam shouted back.

Skorn smiled. "You can keep your lives, and then I'll take you to the end of times so you can witness it all!"

"Brace yourself," Cathal warned Liam, who turned forward and saw what he was planning. He clenched the sides of the cart as Cathal moved right into the path of an oncoming truck.

The truck swerved out of the way, ran right past him, and spun out of control. Skorn quickly dodged the truck as it went past him and smashed directly into one of the cargo trucks, sending all its men flying out. The other truck's driver slammed on his brakes and was able to avoid the pile-up.

Liam looked back. "That changed things quite a bit." He saw only Skorn now behind them, who was now back in control of his bike and getting ready to fire on them once again.

Liam and Skorn engaged in a gun battle as Cathal continued to get closer and closer to the train station. He had just passed a sign that said they were ten kilometers away.

Click, click. Liam looked down at his rifle. It was empty. "I ran out!" Liam yelled.

Cathal quickly reached down and went to hand Liam his own rifle. Liam looked back up to grab the rifle from his hand, but it was too late. The main bike's seat was empty; Cathal had vanished. In that moment, as Liam looked down at his magazine clip, Skorn had sped up to their bike and had apparently knocked Cathal right off the bike.

Cathal was now rolling on the ground, at least fifty yards behind. The bike began to wobble and lose control, and Skorn laughed as he rode side by side with the unstable bike. Liam hopped on the main seat and threw the gun in the sidecar. Regaining control of the bike, he was weaponless and had Skorn right next to him, taunting him.

Cathal stood up, brushing the dirt off him. He miraculously didn't acquire any injuries from the fall. His ears detected something rapidly approaching him from behind. He spun around and immediately jumped up and landed on the front hood of the other cargo truck that had just attempted to run him over.

The two men in the front seats stared back at him in awe as Cathal got down on his fours so that the wind wouldn't knock him off. Cathal stared in through the windshield back at them. The soldier in the passenger seat propped open his window and began to fire at him.

Cathal slid feet first right through the front windshield, smashing the window and landing in between the two men. The soldier in the passenger seat pulled his gun in from the window and attempted to shoot at Cathal, but Cathal answered with several punches to his face, rendering the man into a vegetable state.

The driver screamed and made a poor attempt at hitting Cathal as he opened the passenger door and pushed the limp soldier out of the vehicle. He turned around to divert his attention to the driver, who had now reached for his sidearm. Cathal quickly ripped it from his hand and kicked him repeatedly in the chest and face until he was knocked out as well.

The truck began to swerve uncontrollably. Cathal quickly opened the driver's door and pushed the remaining soldier out. Regaining control of the truck, he stared ahead through the cracked windshield. Liam struggled to fend off Skorn, who continued to toy with him from the other bike, firing at him just close enough to almost hit him. He always missed, though.

Cathal pressed down as hard as he could on the accelerator as the truck sped up, getting closer to them. Skorn hadn't noticed him at all; his focus was all on Liam, who kept trying to reach for his gun and control the bike at the same time. It was a difficult task for Liam, since he had zero practice with driving, except for watching Cathal for those brief moments.

Cathal's truck got close enough to Skorn, bumped the back tire as he aimed at Liam, and threw the gun from Skorn's hands and onto the road.

Liam finally grabbed the gun and started to shoot at Skorn, now helpless, to distract him from Cathal, who was now moving his truck in position for a good hit on Skorn. Cathal slammed on the accelerator one more time and swerved left, smashing into the back wheel of Skorn's bike.

Skorn was sent flying into the woods off the road as the bike smashed into a tree and exploded on impact.

Liam slowed his bike down to allow Cathal to pull ahead. They drove several more minutes until Cathal pulled his truck off to the side of the road. They both got off their vehicles and met up staring at what lay about fifty yards ahead of them—a train yard fenced in with soldiers patrolling on foot all around.

"We made it. The train is still there. Time to formulate a plan," Cathal said and smiled at Liam, patting him on the shoulder.

CHAPTER TWENTY-EIGHT

The sky was a swirl of red and orange as the sun made its final deep plunge into darkness. Cathal and Liam crouched in the brush outside the small fortified train station. This was a military specific train station; there were no waiting platforms for civilians to stand and wait on. The fenced-in area included a watchtower, a small building, and an armored train.

They studied the layout of the station together one last time before the sun dipped finally below the horizon. The watchtower had one man up top, overseeing the whole compound, while five other visible men separately patrolled the area from the ground.

The armored train was completely loaded for an all-out war. "It's like an Armored Rail Cruiser," Cathal whispered to Liam. Liam looked confused and waited for further explanation.

"Basically, while in motion, this train could take out a small army," said Cathal. "See. Look at the different cars."

Cathal pointed as Liam studied the train.

"I see seven train cars, three tanks, three cargo cars, and the lead cab." The cars alternated from the back cargo, the tank, and the lead cab, in that order. Cathal pointed to one of the tanks and continued. "See that tank. It's very similar to the one that we had to deal with in the city, the Tiger I."

"Ehh, we need to use that and not have it used on us," Liam replied.

"Liam, you took the words right out of my mouth," Cathal said. "The stones have to be on there, one of the cargo cars. We need to get on there without being noticed and get the stones."

"What do you suggest we do?" Liam asked, ready for any order Cathal was going to give.

"You wait here," Cathal responded immediately. Liam's facial expression slumped.

"I'm going to take out the guard in the watchtower before we do anything," Cathal explained further. "We need to get their eye out of the sky. Once we do that, I'll signal you from above to come, but you have to be aware of where the other men are on foot!"

"Sounds good. I'll wait. I promise I won't let you down," Liam reassured his cousin.

Cathal nodded at Liam and was off, moving slowly through the brush and crouching so that he did not give away his position to any of the guards.

He got to the edge of the brush, just five feet away from the fence. A guard was walking slowly by him on the other side of the fence along the building. He waited until the guard had rounded the corner out of sight. The guard in the tower had also changed positions and was looking out in the opposite direction away from them.

Cathal came out of hiding and quietly climbed the fence, being careful at the top to avoid the sharp barbed wire. He hopped down and quickly hugged his back to the building. The watchtower guard's view was directly on him now, but Cathal was hidden by the building.

Cathal's ears started to have a heightened sense of his surroundings. He was able to hear the quiet footsteps above him on the tower and on the ground around the base. He could tell the man in the tower had again shifted his attention to the other side. He sensed unwelcoming steps approaching his position from around the corner.

Cathal swung his leg up and struck a guard right in the chin as he started to round the corner. Cathal jumped in quickly, grabbing the unconscious guard before he fell to the ground. He dragged him back around the corner, laying him down just in time before the tower guard turned his attention back to the house.

He turned in again on his newly discovered, superb-hearing capabilities and noticed the guard had already gone to the opposite side of the tower again. Cathal peered around the corner and saw he was clear to move.

Hastily, he made his way to the base of the wooden tower. The ladder was directly on the other side, but he decided not to use this way to make his way up. That would be too suspicious looking, and he knew the guards would probably see him.

He reached up to wrap his hand around a large wooden plank of the structure. The tower was made up of four large wooden pillars, going straight up and forming the tower's corners. Large wooden planks on the side of the tower crossed through each other diagonally from one corner to the next.

Cathal climbed up the side, grabbing one diagonal plank at a time and pulling himself upward until he reached the top. He felt the soldier's presence directly above him as he clung close to the tower to conceal himself.

The soldier made his move to the opposite side of the tower, facing away from him, as Cathal hopped over the edge and onto the platform. He did this more silently than a mouse.

Cathal knocked the soldier out with a strike to the back of his head, bringing him down. Wasting no time, he started taking his own robes off and replaced them with the guard's clothes.

Cathal had only gotten his new shirt and helmet on when he heard a soldier from below shout up to see if he was OK. He felt the tower move a little. A guard was climbing up the ladder. Cathal quickly leaned over the ladder and called down, "Alles ist gut."

The soldier stared up at him for a moment. Cathal wondered if he had said the German phrase correctly—which meant "all is well"—or if the guard could see that it wasn't his fellow soldier. It was dark, and there was no light on them to really tell what their faces looked like. Cathal didn't take his eyes off the soldier, nor did the soldier take his off him.

The soldier took one last stare up at the motionless Cathal and then nodded, stepping back down off the ladder.

Cathal sighed with relief and got back to work, replacing all his clothing with the appropriate Nazi uniform and picking up his rifle.

He moved toward the place where he had left Liam. He could spot Liam just barely in the brush. Cathal examined the surrounding area by scouting out the base from above to see where the other soldiers were at that particular moment. He spotted three of the soldiers continuing to patrol their areas, and he could still see the soldier he had encountered on the ground, still knocked out. There was one soldier still missing from view, but the area seemed clear, so he motioned for Liam to climb the fence.

Liam made his way out of the brush and climbed the fence, carefully avoiding the barbed wire at the top. He landed gently and then disappeared from Cathal's view behind the building.

He waited to see Liam again. Seconds ticked by, but still there was no sign. Worried, he scanned the area around to see where the soldiers currently were, and then he looked back to Liam's hiding spot. He still wasn't in sight. Cathal heard a thud. He immediately jumped over the top railing of the tower and fell two stories to the ground, where he landed perfectly.

He ran over to the corner of the building and peered around the edge. Liam walked toward him, smiling, rifle in hand. A Nazi soldier was facedown behind him.

"Well, I just didn't have time to get changed like you," Liam said and smirked as he looked at Cathal's new uniform.

"Nice job, but you need to change as well. We don't know how many of them we will encounter, and if we don't cause alarm, all the better."

Liam took off his own clothes and the soldier's and changed into Nazi attire to match with Cathal's.

Cathal got on his knees and crawled along the outside wall to the edge of the building, closest to the train. Liam followed right behind. Peering around the corner, they both felt that the train's monstrous scale placed them both in an intimidated daze.

"This looks a lot bigger than before in the fields," whispered Liam.

"You're right. Still, it's the same plan," responded Cathal. "We're going to infiltrate the train. Hopefully, there's no commotion, considering we are now in proper uniform. We should be able to find the stones, which are probably located in one of the cargo holds, and use the Tiger tank, if needed."

Liam pointed out the other two tanks. "What about them?"

"If we have to get in a tank and use them, we must get into the closest available and hope for the best. If we don't, then we've already lost."

"Tiger Tank. Understood." Liam smiled in anticipation but then gulped from nerves.

"Nicht bewegen," a voice said from behind.

They both turned around to see an armed Nazi pointing his rifle directly at Cathal.

Liam leaned toward Cathal, "What did he say?"

"He said, 'Don't move,'" Cathal responded. They were both in a terrible position to do anything productive to get out of this situation. Cathal needed to be on his feet, but getting there in time would certainly cause too much alarm to the guard who was just a few feet away.

"Aufstehen. Hände hinter dem Kopf," commanded the guard. He used his gun to motion an upward movement.

"Stand up, and put your hands behind your head," Cathal translated to Liam.

They both stood up and placed their hands behind their heads. Cathal could tell this was a new soldier; standing up gave them way too much opportunity to fight back. This now became the absolute perfect situation for him. Cathal was within striking distance of the guard and, hopefully, would be able to maneuver quick enough to gain the upper hand.

The guard went for his whistle to alert his fellow comrades, but before he could get to blow into it, Cathal's body went into one fluid motion. His body left the ground and performed a backflip kick, striking the soldier across the face. The soldier fell to the ground instantly, immobilized.

"Ugh! So much to learn!" Liam demanded in a loud whisper.

"Shh, when we have time," Cathal replied as he grabbed the unconscious soldier's rifle, handgun, and knife. He wrapped the second rifle over his shoulders, handed the handgun to Liam, and placed the knife in its sheath in the back of his own pants.

A voice shouted out orders nearby the train. The voice was eerily recognizable and immediately caught their attention. Skorn came running into the area, shouting at the remaining two soldiers to board the train. He looked bruised and battered but completely full of energy.

The train began to get very loud and move very slowly. It was departing. The two remaining soldiers got on some of the cars from the back, while Skorn climbed on top of the back cargo car; he started running forward, jumping from one car to the next.

The train began to pick up more speed, moving farther away from them. "We've got to go now!" commanded Cathal.

Liam and Cathal bolted from the safety of the building and sprinted for the departing train out in the open.

As they closed the distance, a soldier, spotting them, poked his head into view from one of the cars. He shouted to alert the others and started to fire at them.

Bullets flew past their heads and hit the ground beside them as they closed the gap with the train, which began to pick up even more speed.

"Come on!" Cathal shouted, dodging another bullet and firing back at the soldier.

They edged closer, continuing to dodge more bullets. The back car was now within reach. Cathal extended his left hand to grab ahold of the last car's railing and was successful. He propped himself up on the ledge. Still holding on with his left, he reached out his right hand to grab ahold of Liam. Liam got ahold of his hand and heaved himself up onto the ledge of the car.

"So much for getting on unnoticed." Liam struggled to pull the words out of his mouth. He was breathing extremely heavily.

The shouts from the soldiers began to close in on them.

CHAPTER TWENTY-NINE

Liam pushed himself up into a standing position to join Cathal. "What's the plan now?" Liam asked. "They're coming for us."

"There should be two stones on board. They're the last two, the Sky one and Viktor's center joining piece," Cathal responded. "We need to—"

"Get up here now!" Cathal was interrupted by shouting from above, on top of one of the train cars.

"One moment..." Cathal steadily crept up the ladder to glance over the top of the train car. Skorn was waiting for him as if a tiger ready to pounce on its prey.

Cathal hopped down to address the situation with Liam. "It's Skorn. I'm going to take him on up top. You go through the train cars and search thoroughly for the stones. They have to be here. Skorn wouldn't be here if they weren't."

"I will find them!" Liam assured Cathal.

Cathal placed his hand on Liam's shoulder. "Look for a type of marking indicating where the stones are. When I was in Chicago, the crate with the stone had a special marking on the side. You've got this."

Cathal turned his back to him and climbed up to meet Skorn above the train car.

"Well now. Isn't this fun?" Skorn smirked as he walked toward him, arms stretched out to each side and holding a machete in his right hand.

"Give me the stones, Skorn! You don't know what the Tarnok are truly capable of!" Cathal pleaded as he moved forward. "We are all going to die!"

Skorn continued to smile. He was now about ten feet from Cathal. "I don't need this to deal with you." After saying this, Skorn hurled the machete off the moving train and into the woods.

"I'm not going to die," said Skorn. "I'm going to be their savior, the one who ensures that they come into their rightful power! I'll be at the Tarnok's side when they destroy the Elluna, then Elluna's Guard, and then finally everyone else who won't bow to Terranos and won't join the Tarnen!"

"You're mad! The Tarnok will bring about the end of the world! They don't care for any human beings!" Cathal pleaded. This talk only angered Skorn, however.

"Enough talk. It's been a pleasure," Skorn said and then threw himself at Cathal, at what appeared to be twice the rate of the train's motion, and clotheslined Cathal onto the floor of the train.

Cathal lay helpless on his back, trying to catch the wind that was knocked clear out of him. Skorn circled him above, striking a blow with his foot to Cathal's ribs.

"Get up! I want a fight!" shouted Skorn.

Another kick to the ribs jolted Cathal back to life. He rolled onto his stomach and stood up. Skorn took a step back and said, "That's it, get up. I'm going to end you now. No more games."

"This world is going to survive, and the Tarnok are going to be sent back, never to return again!" Cathal stormed after Skorn, throwing punches at an alarming speed. Skorn countered with an equal amount of blocks.

They each exchanged devastating blows, almost knocking each other off balance. Skorn's cocky attitude transitioned to a moderately concerned composure. Normally, fights for Skorn would normally begin to slow down with a depletion of energy; however, this fight intensified with each strike. They both seemed to have a limitless supply of endurance. This fight was fueled purely by their hatred for one another.

Cathal circled around Skorn, with his back to the front of the train. Both were breathing heavily but ready to continue the onslaught. Skorn's eyes widened, and he ducked. Cathal turned his head to see what he was looking at, but it was too late. An oncoming tree branch connected with Cathal's back, sending him flying into the air and off the side of the train.

Skorn stood up and walked over to the edge where Cathal had disappeared. Hands clenching on the side rail, Cathal held on for his life. His legs swung back and forth, knocking into the side of the train. Skorn stared down at him, smiling, and moved closer to the edge. Cathal looked up into his eyes. All he could see was darkness and flames.

Liam entered the first train car. Both sides of the car had generic boxes stacked up to the ceiling, with the word *Munition* stamped on the sides. He made his way through, propping open boxes that were on the top of each stack. All he could find in each were different types of ammunition. Liam slammed the top down on a box, disappointed and aggravated. "Nothing here," he said and sighed, exiting the first car.

Outside, he could hear Cathal and Skorn fighting from above. He carefully walked across the link connecting the two cars in the back. He glanced down at the railroad beneath him; they were moving by so fast that it was all a blur. The sounds of fighting above reminded him of what he was doing. He refocused and entered the second car.

This car had wooden crates stacked up on each side. A walkway went down its middle, but there was nothing written on any of the crates' sides. He walked over to one of the crates. He heard a slam on top of the roof and some more pounding. "They are really going at it up there," Liam said to himself as he opened the first crate.

The crate was filled with straw; nothing else. Confused, he stuck his hands deep into the crate and felt around, hoping to find some stones. Nothing but straw and hay.

"You know, you two should really just give up already!" a voice said startling Liam.

Liam turned to his right and saw a man walk out from behind one of the stacks of crates. Monstrous in size and shirtless, he was at least a foot taller than Liam and more muscular than anyone he had ever laid eyes upon. The soldier stood towering at the end of the car, just staring at him from a distance and grinning.

"I don't have time for this!" Liam shouted, and then he fired several rounds from his rifle at the man's chest. The sound that came from the bullet impact was metallic as if he had fired at the side of a tank. The bullets connected with his chest and immediately fell to the floor. The enormous soldier remained standing and started to laugh. The skin where the bullets had impacted him was now of a metallic tint.

"You can't hurt me. No one can," the man said, and then he ran toward Liam, who, in turn, threw a nearby crate at him. The crate connected with the man's arm, causing his skin around his arm to become metallic. He swung with his metal arm, but Liam ducked and ran past him. His arm continued to gyrate; it went through another wooden crate with ease.

Liam turned around to see where his attacker was. He was pulling his arm out of the crushed crate. He stood leaning in the direction of his metallic arm; it seemed to be much heavier on his body now. Liam had an idea: he picked up another crate and threw it at his other arm.

Cathal hung from the side of the train car, staring up at Skorn, who had already started his victory celebration. Cathal looked down; they were now on a bridge way up high. If he fell, he would surely die. He looked out to see where the train was heading; all he could see were the monstrous mountains, the Alps, a view that, at any other time, would be something to stop and marvel at for several hours. But he had no time for this now.

The feeling of crushing overwhelmed his left hand as it fell underneath Skorn's boot. "It's over, Cathal! And before I end you, I want to tell you something!" Skorn smiled more as he pressed down with his boot on his hand some more.

As Skorn was about to inform Cathal of the terrible news, a loud explosion formed farther up the train. Skorn turned in the direction of the blast. One of the cargo cars was up in flames and almost blown to bits. The Tiger I tank up front's main gun rotated slightly and fired again, hitting the middle tank and blowing it off the platform it was on. The middle tank fell into the unknown below.

Skorn screamed in German at the tank and turned back around to center his attention once more on

Cathal, but Cathal wasn't there anymore. Skorn frantically turned in different directions, searching for him, but before he could turn all the way around, he was thrown off the cargo car and on top of the tank on the next platform. Cathal hopped on top of the tank and ambled toward the staggered Skorn.

The manned tank fired another round at Cathal, who dove out of the way and braced his fall by clinging onto the barrel of the tank. The barrel had been positioned so that it hung over the side of the tracks. Suspended, Cathal looked down. If he let go, he would fall hundreds of feet to his death.

Another round fired. Cathal swung himself further out to the end of the barrel, dodging the round. Skorn jumped off the tank and made his way up to the hatch of the manned tank and banged on the hatch.

Back in the train car, Liam threw another box at the soldier's fully metallic legs. The box shattered instantaneously into small pieces. Liam had tactically attacked every part of the now clunky metal man. He backed up into the side wall of the cargo car.

"Come on! You big hunk of metal. Come at me!" Liam provoked the soldier, who fell for his trick and dove directly at him. Liam waited until the very last second to dive out of the way. The soldier dove and connected with the wall, smashing right through it and disappearing.

Liam ran back to the hole in the train and looked outside. There was no sign of the soldier. He looked down to the ground hundreds of feet below. The metallic body was falling at a rapid pace. "I guess I won," Liam said to himself.

Liam quickly ran to the exit of the car and opened the door to see Cathal hanging from the end of the tank's barrel, swinging and dodging ammunition rounds.

"I'm here, but there's no stones!" Liam yelled at Cathal as he climbed up on the top of the tank. He saw Skorn in the distance on top of the firing tank. The hatch had opened, and Skorn reached down, pulling a Nazi soldier out and throwing him overboard. He then dropped down into the tank and closed the hatch. This was a good indication that Liam should do the same.

The train had now gotten off the bridge and was now traveling over level land on both sides.

"Liam, get in there, and give me cover fire! Distract Skorn, while I look for the stones!" Cathal commanded Liam. Liam then climbed down into the tank and rotated the barrel over the train so Cathal could safely get off.

Skorn's tank then did something that they did not expect. Instead of firing at them, it veered off the train and began following the train alongside it to the left.

Liam rotated the barrel to fire on Skorn, but Skorn's hit Liam's tank before he could get his shot off, rocking the tank but not rendering it useless. Liam repositioned the barrel and fired on Skorn and hit the tank, but the round deflected, smashing apart half a tree in the woods behind it.

Cathal moved through the half-blown-up cargo car in front, trying to avoid Skorn's detection; then he moved onto the car where the tank had been.

Liam finished reloading the main barrel and saw Skorn fire a round at Cathal, who dove again, barely dodging the bullet.

Liam fired another missile at the back of Skorn's tank, and it connected perfectly. His tank slowed down to a complete stop. Smoke rapidly flowed out the hole Liam had blown open as the train moved past it. Liam screamed in victorious fashion.

Liam climbed out of the tank and stood on top. He watched as he saw Cathal enter the lead car. His victorious celebration ceased immediately with the thing that caught his eye next.

A couple hundred yards down the track, three Tiger tanks blocked the railroad; their barrels were all aimed right at the lead car.

A loud explosion occurred as all three tanks fired on the lead car with Cathal inside. The lead car was hit, and the explosion sent it directly into the air and off the tracks into the woods.

Liam was knocked off the top of the tank. He wrapped his arms around the barrel as the rest of the train was pulled off the tracks and went crashing into the woods.

CHAPTER THIRTY

Three Nazi jeeps pulled up to the tanks, blocking the railroad. Twelve soldiers jumped out of their vehicles and stared in awe at the derailed train on its side. They could only see one half of the train from their viewpoint; the other half was somewhere in the woods. Fire and smoke mixed with the darkness and made it very hard to see what was left of the main car in the woods.

A high-ranking officer started to shout out orders. "I need six of you men to retrieve the precious cargo that is located in that front car. It's a small chest!"

The soldiers looked at each other, troubled.

"Do it now! And don't come back until you have it!" the high-ranking officer commanded. The men hurried into formation and cautiously headed into the woods toward what was left of the front car.

"I wonder where Skorn—" the officer began saying but was interrupted.

A loud shrieking sound came from above; the men who stayed back looked into the air, blinded from the bolt of light that came crashing down out of the darkness. Whatever it was, it smashed directly into one of the military jeeps, blowing it up into pieces.

A shooting pain started in Cathal's leg and spread throughout his body, bringing him back to awareness. He looked down at his leg. He was pinned down with a sharp piece of metal from the wall, pressing into his upper thigh.

He attempted to maneuver out of this muscle-tearing hold, but the pain was too severe, and the metal seemed to dig deeper into his thigh with every attempt.

A sound coming from outside the train car silenced him and ceased all movement. Someone was trying to get into the car. Cathal pressed back into the wall to hide from the worst possible encounter. He hoped it was Liam.

Skorn's head poked in as he pushed the rubble out of the way and stumbled into the train car. He frantically threw to the side anything that was in his way, searching the destroyed train car for something. Cathal kept quiet and out of sight, even though the pain was excruciating.

"Dammit! Where is it?" Skorn mumbled to himself in frustration as he pushed some more debris around. "Ah, there."

Skorn reached down and picked up a small chest. Without a second thought, he quickly brushed it off and left the train.

Cathal went right back, trying to get free. He pressed against the metal sticking out of his thigh to push himself away. He made some progress moving a bit but not enough. Blood gushed more and more out of his leg as he continued to attempt to break free.

The blood loss was so much that Cathal lost the physical ability to even continue functioning. He slowly faded into unconsciousness.

Moments later, Liam pushed through the same entrance that Skorn had just left. "Cathal!" Liam whispered as loudly as he could. "Cathal!" Liam peered around each corner, looking for his cousin.

His eyes traveled a little further into the car and spotted Cathal, lifeless. Liam rushed over to him and smacked him in the face. Cathal came to.

"Skorn, he took the chest—"

"Cathal, stop talking, and let me help you out of here." Liam studied the metal protruding out of Cathal's leg.

"He took the chest. It had the stones in it." Cathal fought for every word that came out of his mouth. More blood escaped from his wound.

Kyle Gurkovich

"I know. I saw him come out and waited for him to leave. I saw the direction he was headed for, but we have to get you out first."

Liam reached down and picked up a broken-off piece of wood from a crate and said, "You're going to need to bite down on this."

Liam placed the piece in Cathal's mouth, who bit down.

"I'm sorry. This is really going to hurt." Liam grabbed the piece of metal from underneath and pulled away and up. Cathal bit down harder and harder; his eyes bulged, but the wood kept his screams muffled. Liam pulled harder. He could feel and hear Cathal's leg muscles tearing. His eyes widened even more; Cathal's face, now completely red, was covered in veins.

Liam gave one final pull, throwing himself backward. The pain was immense. Cathal bit down so hard that he broke the wood in half. They did it; the metal was out.

In moments, Cathal's breathing slowed down from its rapid pace. Liam stared at his wound on his thigh and couldn't believe his eyes. With each moment, it began to close and heal.

"What is going on?" Liam could barely get the words out of his mouth.

Cathal was in no more pain, and his breathing returned to a calm tempo. He stared down at his wound—which, just moments ago, was overflowing with blood and could have ended all function in his leg forever—but saw nothing but skin in its place. It was as if it had never happened. If Liam's jaw could roll to the floor, it would have.

"Thank you, Liam, but we have no time to question what just happened. Skorn is way ahead of us by now. We've got to catch up to him!"

"You are something else, cousin!"

Cathal chuckled, got up on his own, and followed Liam as they exited the train.

Cathal questioned his whereabouts. "How did we get into the middle of the woods?"

"You were basically blown up by several tanks." Liam pointed farther into the woods. "He was headed in that direction."

"Let's go then." Cathal rushed forward, and Liam followed. They moved only several feet before Cathal stopped abruptly in place.

"Get down!" shouted Cathal. Bullets shot right past their heads as they dropped to the ground.

The six Nazi soldiers who were ordered to find the chest were now fixated on their location about forty yards away.

Cathal peered through the brush; they were getting closer. "We have got to run," said Cathal, and he pulled Liam up with him, and they began to run.

"We are always running!" Liam screamed.

The Nazi soldiers fired more shots that just missed the two of them. A loud explosion shook the ground and almost knocked Liam off his feet. Cathal turned his head as he ran and saw giant flashes light up the night sky, followed by explosions coming from behind the soldiers. The soldiers turned around to see what was going on; it was a huge firefight. They hesitated to go back, but they had orders.

"What's going on?" Liam shouted, out of breath, as he continued to try to keep pace with Cathal. He had to keep avoiding random ditches and tree roots. "I don't understand. You almost lost your leg, and I'm struggling to keep up with you!"

Cathal turned around again and peered through the openings in the trees. He saw more flashing lights coming from a small flying object. He could see the tanks firing and missing at whatever it was in the sky, moving around like an annoying fly you couldn't get rid of.

"It must be Gabriel!" yelled Cathal.

Liam peered back and saw the soldiers still in pursuit but losing ground.

Cathal ran by a tree, and something caught something in his eye. A branch from the tree had a piece of ripped cloth hanging from it. It looked exactly like what Skorn had been wearing. This eased his already-stressful situation. They were at least still going in the right direction. Cathal stated, "We must be close."

The woods ceased as they came to a complete stop. In front of them was a grassy field. Skorn had disappeared into the thick brush. "This may be our only chance," Cathal whispered.

"Why do we always go through grassy fields?" Liam commented on the situation at hand.

Cathal and Liam quietly entered the thick brush in pursuit of Skorn, while the small group of soldiers pursued behind them. This situation was very reminiscent of the time Liam and Cathal were in China, except this time they were the ones chasing after Skorn, not the other way around.

On they pushed through the thick grass, clandestine in manner. They could hear the obnoxious soldiers from behind. They had just entered into the brush. The real issue was that they couldn't hear Skorn. Had he already left this time period? That question burned in Cathal's mind.

"Stop," whispered Cathal. Cathal pressed his hand against Liam's chest, forcing him to abruptly end his walking. "Notice that—"

"I can't hear anything," Liam replied.

They looked around. In the darkness of the night, they could barely see more than one foot in front of themselves in this brush.

"Where did—"

Cathal slammed his hand over Liam's mouth, silencing him. Cathal readied himself for an immediate attack.

Before Liam could figure out what was happening, Skorn appeared through the brush, diving for Liam and knocking him over, hitting him with the chest. Liam was immediately knocked out cold. Cathal spun around. Skorn stood there, holding the chest in both hands.

Cathal kicked him straight in the head. The chest left the snug grip of his hands and fell to the ground, but Skorn was only slightly shook up. Skorn went right for Cathal. They exchanged many blows. The brush around them started to break and fall with every attack.

Skorn made Cathal flinch with a fake punch from the left but quickly grabbed him from the right, slamming him to the ground. He sat directly on top of Cathal, knees pressing down on both of his biceps and both hands wrapped violently around his neck. Skorn squeezed with all his might.

Cathal struggled to breathe and fought against Skorn's knees to break free, but the weight Skorn put on him and the loss of oxygen rendered him helpless. He started to lose all hope. His vision began to fade.

Liam came to and saw Skorn on top of Cathal and choking his cousin. Quietly, he struggled to his feet and picked up the chest. He moved over to Skorn, who was so engrossed in ending Cathal's life that he had no sense of what was going on around him, and swung, connecting the chest to Skorn's head. The immediate impact sent him to the ground.

Cathal's energy snapped right back, and his breathing rapidly regained itself.

"Come on, get up," said Liam, and he pulled Cathal to his feet and picked up the chest. Hearing their voices, Cathal and Liam knew that the soldiers were now only a few feet away but were still invisible through the dense brush.

"Let's go," Liam said, pushing through the brush, away from a motionless Skorn and the soldiers, while Cathal followed.

"Up ahead, Liam. Get to that forest line," Cathal said and pointed, now fully aware of his surroundings. His breathing was now perfectly fine.

They made it through the remainder of the field to the forest line and into the woods about a hundred yards before they stopped. Liam placed the chest down on the ground.

"I still don't understand your leg and how it healed, and how you were just choked out but are completely fine right now," Liam said to Cathal.

"I have no idea either. Maybe Crowley can answer some of these questions," Cathal replied. "Help me open this chest."

They struggled trying to pry open the chest together with their bare hands. It was an extremely odd chest with no latch or means of opening it.

Wind began to swirl about them, and then something came crashing down beside them. Gabriel appeared.

"Sorry, I had gotten distracted with some resistance." Gabriel smiled as if this were all no big deal. "I sense that inside this chest are several of the God Stones. Step aside."

"Thank you so much for your help again, Gabriel," Cathal said and graciously moved to the side; Liam followed.

Gabriel gently kicked the chest from the side, and it popped right open.

Kyle Gurkovich

They both shook their head at Gabriel, who smiled and shrugged in return.

They all hovered over the chest. Inside lay the last two of the God Stones. Both were of a deep black obsidian. One had three wavy lines cut by a lightning bolt, and the other one was of a perfect circle.

"Sky and Viktor's joining stone," Gabriel added.

"I believe it's time to gather all the stones." Relief flowed through Cathal's body and his words. "We did it. We accomplished the impossible."

Cathal picked up both stones. Liam and Gabriel placed their hands on Cathal's shoulders. He closed his eyes, and with the flash of a blue light, they were gone.

Footsteps approached a limp Skorn. One of the soldiers knelt down and tapped Skorn until he woke up. Skorn flipped his body upward into a standing defensive position. He quickly realized who it was and regained his composure.

"Sir, what do we do now? What are your orders?" a Nazi asked Skorn.

"First, give me a gun," Skorn replied.

The soldier pulled out a Browning pistol from his right holster and handed it to him.

Without hesitation, Skorn rapidly shot all six soldiers in the head before the first could hit the ground.

Skorn began to breath heavy as they all fell simultaneously to the ground. His face rapidly went from a pale white to red in moments. His rapid breathing turned into silent anger. His face seemed to be boiling over with rage, until he let out a giant scream.

CHAPTER THIRTY-ONE

The pitch-black forest lit up with a flash of blue light. Liam, Cathal, and Gabriel appeared above the small hill where they had stowed the other God Stones in secret.

Cathal handed the two remaining God Stones to Liam to hold. Liam's face lit up in wonderment and awe as he gazed into the darkness. No matter how many times his eyes fell upon any of the stones, it was always the same reaction. Gabriel laughed at Liam's astonishment and shook his head. Cathal jumped down the small hill and crept underneath, into the hole, to recover the other three remaining stones.

Cathal came out from the hole with the three other stones cradled in his arms. "Before we go, I'd like to see Keela."

"Not possible," Gabriel responded before Cathal could almost finish his statement.

"I don't understand. We don't know what is coming next. What if this is the last possible chance I have to see her?" His tone was oozing with agitation.

"It's not a wise decision. Every moment wasted is another moment Skorn could ruin," Liam added his own thoughts, siding against Cathal for once.

"Listen, you two. I'm going to see her now. And that's..." Cathal paused a moment. "And that's..." Cathal's head started to spin. "And that's..." His body started to stagger, and he fell to the ground.

Gabriel moved in with lightning speed, catching him before he hit the ground. "We don't have time to waste, but we can't function without you being well rested and ready for what is to come. You both need rest."

Cathal stood upright. "You're right. I'll see her after we've placed the God Stones together at the end date."

Gabriel pointed to the ground before them and shot a bolt of lightning through his fingertips into it. The lightning created a warm fire that illuminated the dark forest around them. "Rest. I'll watch over you two and the stones," said Gabriel. "When you wake up, we shall be on our way."

Liam and Cathal placed the stones together in the dirt next to Gabriel, in an effort to form the perfect circle they would need at the end date. All the other God Stones were on the outside, surrounding Viktor's stone in the middle. They both lay down next to the fire and closed their eyes. The warmth of the flames soothed them, both physically and mentally, causing them to fall asleep immediately.

Gabriel watched over them and the stones for several hours before they awoke again.

Cathal pulled out the scroll that Crowley had given him with the dates. It was only several days ago that Crowley had given him this scroll, but he felt so much wiser and more seasoned than the young man who had entered Crowley's hut eight days ago. He had endured a lot in that time. "The last date on here is for the twenty-first of August in the year 2023."

"Where do we go for this?" Liam asked.

"I don't know," explained Cathal. "For some reason, anytime I try to travel past this date, it won't work. The bracelet seems to go dead. I have no clue where I need to go."

"Where *we* need to go," Liam corrected Cathal, who smiled and nodded in return. "You aren't doing this alone."

"It doesn't matter where we go. We just need to go somewhere then. Pick a place, and put the stones together. Viktor and the rest of the Elluna should come and regain their powers," Gabriel noted.

Cathal crept back inside the hole where he kept the stones hidden. He came back out with a leather sack and started placing the stones in the sack. "Let's quickly gather what we need and head out," he said.

Everyone agreed. Gabriel placed his hand over the immaculate fire, and the flames were sucked up into his hand, disappearing into empty air. There wasn't much to take. Cathal and Liam were still in their Nazi uniforms. They both used the knives they'd acquired to slice off anything that indicated they were Nazis.

Cathal lifted up the sack filled with the God Stones and said, "Let's go." Liam and Gabriel each placed a hand on one of his shoulders. The dark forest lit with a bright blue one last time before they vanished from it for, possibly, the last time.

CHAPTER THIRTY-TWO

The sun was shining, and there was not a cloud in the sky when the three of them appeared on a brick walkway. Liam was in awe of the beautiful view before him: the New York City skyline and, a little to the side, the Statue of Liberty. Several people walked past them on the walkway but didn't take any notice of them appearing out of nowhere, thanks to the music blasting in their ears from their headphones.

"Welcome to Liberty State Park in New Jersey. In front of you is the most influential city in the entire world," Cathal explained.

Liam was impressed, but Gabriel wasn't. "We need to get started. Maybe one day we can enjoy views like this, but it's not this day," Gabriel insisted.

Cathal placed the sack on the ground and started to take out the God Stones one by one.

An old lady walking by with her small Boxer puppy had a disturbed look on her face as she passed them. "Reenactors..." she said. "Two old army men and a weirdo in a Greek toga. What next?"

Cathal placed the God Stones together on the brick walkway, like pieces in a puzzle. Once he placed the fourth one down, they magically locked together. Each of the four elements were perfectly shaped to the quarter size of a doughnut. The top left bore four triangular tips, representing the mountains, or earth. The top right had four wave lines, representing water. The bottom left had the shape of flames, representing fire. The bottom right showed wavy lines with a lightning bolt going through the middle, signifying the sky.

Cathal picked up the last stone; it was impeccably crafted into a perfect circle. The deep blackness he stared into shifted to a design, and on the stone another perfect circle appeared with a sword going through it.

"The circle represents all the power together joining as one, and the sword represents the might of all of the Elluna's power when the stones are combined," Gabriel said. "It's time, Cathal. Place it in the middle."

Cathal carefully placed the final stone in the center of the other four, pressing down until it locked in place. He stood up and took a step back. The newly formed stone started to shake a little, but the shaking quickly faded away. They all stared at the stones, waiting for something to happen.

But nothing happened.

"Did Crowley mention anything else?" Liam asked. "Was there something we needed to say?"

"He didn't say anything," Cathal answered. "I assumed that when we placed them together, they would just activate."

"I couldn't tell you either. I assumed the same," Gabriel added, confusion spreading across his face.

Rumblings from the sky above caused them to look upward. The clear skies were now darkened with black clouds, which blanketed everything their eyes could see.

"This can't be good." Liam's face now showed the beginnings of horror.

Suddenly, red lightning splintered the dark sky. Rumblings shook the ground they stood on. They all had to brace themselves as the ground continued to shake, and the lightning continued to spread across the sky and amplify by the second.

"Come on, work!" Cathal yelled at the stones.

"Oh my *God*, look!" Liam pointed back toward the sky. All the clouds disappeared, but there was no more sun and daylight; it was pure darkness.

Another roar shook the ground. The sky lit up again, but it wasn't light from the sun. Large fiery comets came crashing down, making their descent into the earth's atmosphere. The world's impending doom appeared to be upon it.

The ground still shook. The God Stones started to separate, and the magical bond that held them so tightly together was no more. Useless, the stones rolled around until they rested on their sides.

"It's them—the Tarnok. Were we too late?" The cold words struggled to leave Gabriel's mouth.

"Where are they? Where's Viktor? Where's the Elluna?" Cathal asked as he frantically stared at his failure crashing to the surface, the end of the world. His eyes were completely orange from the glow of the Tarnok's return. "Where did we go wrong?"

Made in the USA
Middletown, DE
04 November 2015